PICTURES FROM PARADISE

JACKI KELLY

ALSO BY JACKI KELLY

THE SWEET ROAD SERIES

The Sweet Road Home

The Sweet Road to Love

The Sweet Road Back

DATING JUST GOT SERIOUS

Blind Date

One Date at a Time

Date Me

A Single Date

Speed Date

Done with Dating

Dating Just Got Serious – Box Set

WOMEN'S FICTION

Packed and Ready to Go

Going Backwards

ALL ABOUT BLISS

A Season of Bliss

JOIN THE JACKI KELLY NEWSLETTER

at

Jackikelly.com!

So you can stay tuned to new releases, guest appearances and events and prizes. She's always giving away something.

PICTURES FROM PARADISE

Jacki Kelly

Copyright 2018 by Kelly, Jacki

ISBN: 978-1-9422202-23-3

First Edition Electronic April 2018

Published by Yobachi Publishing, LLC

❀ Created with Vellum

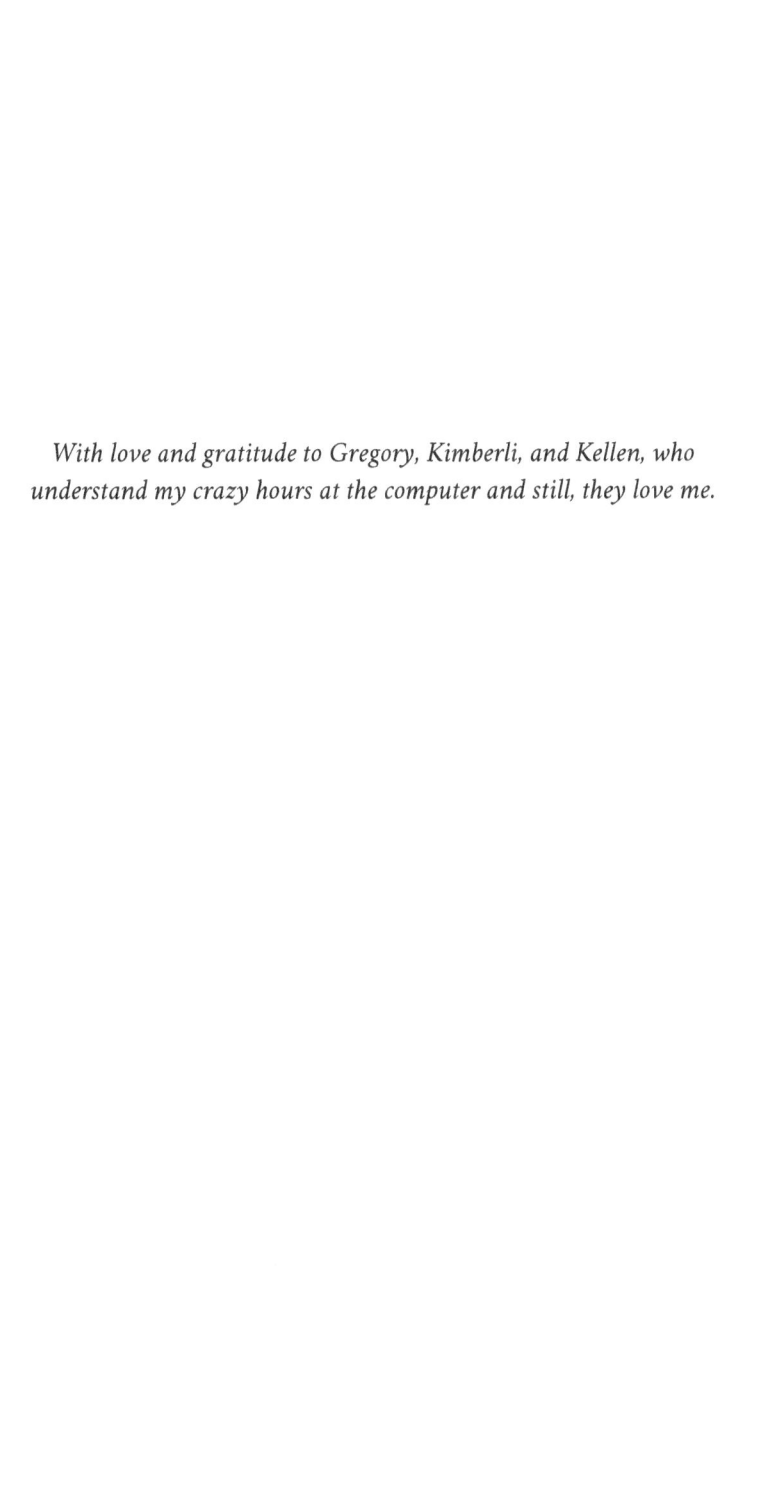

With love and gratitude to Gregory, Kimberli, and Kellen, who understand my crazy hours at the computer and still, they love me.

CHAPTER 1

*O*livia Sika exited the warehouse with her two assistants who were more like friends than employees. But she didn't keep them informed about all the horrible details going on in her life right now. Some things were better left unsaid.

She pulled her sunglasses from her bag and slipped them on. The air was warm and muggy, typical for a late spring day in New York City, and had her dress clinging to the moisture on her back.

"Are you sure you don't want company tonight?" Ajay drilled her with a stare.

She and Ajay had gone out on two dates, but if she wanted everyone to know her as a professional photographer, sleeping with the set assistant didn't fit into the business plan. Not to mention, she needed a competent assistant more than she needed a boyfriend. Besides, Ajay was a playboy, something else she didn't need.

"Yes, let's have drinks. We can go to your favorite place on Roosevelt Avenue." Gwen's head bobbed up and down her curly hair bouncing.

"Guys, I'm exhausted. All I want to do is go home and examine the shots I took today. Gwen, I know you have something more exciting to do than to board the train and take that long-ass ride to Queens." Oliva waved them away. "I'll see you tomorrow. Don't forget we've got to be there early to catch the morning sun since we're shooting outside."

"Sure thing, boss lady," Ajay tapped the screen of his phone while trying to keep up with them.

"Don't call me boss. You know I hate that."

Without waiting for him to reply, she made her way up 29th Street with Gwen at her side and Ajay a few paces behind.

"Wow, you were harsh on Ajay," Gwen whispered.

"He keeps calling me that, and I've told him to stop a hundred times. It's almost like he does it because he knows I don't like it."

"He wouldn't do that. Remember, he called me Toots for several weeks when he started working with us?"

Olivia chuckled. "I remember."

Gwen was the first person who'd answered her ad for a make-up artist and stylist assistant. It hadn't taken the two of them long to realize they had more in common than being employer and employee. They were more like long-lost sisters who had finally found each other. They both wore their hair natural, and while Gwen's hair hung in waves to her shoulders, Olivia's hair was black and curly, resembling a profusion of dark clouds around her face. They competed to see who could wear the most outlandish outfits. Today Gwen won. Her tiny denim shorts and red cowboy boots were a stark contrast to her white sequined tank. Olivia looked down at her silk spaghetti strapped sundress that was so short it almost exposed her butt.

Gwen pointed to Olivia's feet. "Oh, look. Your toes are

painted the same color as your dress. I bet you spent all day looking for yellow polish."

"Yeah, but we both know you nailed it today." Olivia stopped walking.

"Girl, you've gotta come better than matching nail polish if you want to run with this sista." Gwen waved her goodbye and continued toward 34th Street.

Ajay stepped up beside her and shoved his phone into his pants pocket. "Any plans for the weekend?"

She had to look up at him because he was as tall as he was good-looking. Women liked to flirt with him, and he enjoyed the attention. "I've been too busy to think about the weekend," she said. "If I'm lucky, I'll finish my laundry."

The sidewalk was thick with tourists and the rush-hour crowd. Gwen and Ajay's concerns were reassuring, but they were going overboard with the idea that they had to protect her. She'd made enough changes in her life to keep her safe.

Trying to determine who was making her life miserable was useless. Every time she did, nothing came up that made sense. There were no bad break-ups. The only one left heartbroken had been her. There were no grudges that needed a resolution because she avoided confrontation, even when it wasn't in her best interest. There were no social media wars where she'd waged battle. She didn't owe anyone money, nor had she seduced anyone's husband or lover. What was happening was just one of those things that would fade when the stalker grew tired of her boring life. The last time the stalker had left her fifty-four voicemail messages in two hours, the police had told her there wasn't anything they could do.

Before descending the stairs to the subway, she looked around for anyone who'd been behind her for too long. Another new habit. The man in the gray suit had been behind her for several blocks. She pulled her whistle from her camera bag, just in case the man followed her down the stairs

"You can't keep glancing over your shoulder," Ajay said.

"It's a habit now." The guy in the suit was nowhere in sight. She eased the air out of her lungs. Living this way was crazy. How long could she go on like this before she broke?

The heated underground was as oppressive as it was outside. Perspiration dripped down the center of her back. She squeezed her eyes shut for a moment. Instead of focusing on all the things that weren't going right, she needed to think about all the stuff that was finally turning in her favor. The assignment from *Beauty Bar Magazine* was enough to make her happy for months. The check would keep her and the company afloat for a while. The next time her father called to brag about one of her sibling's accomplishments, she'd do a little bragging of her own.

The crowd on the platform pressed forward. Everyone looked down the track at the train's approaching lights. The train came to a stop, and Oliva kept up with the momentum of the other passengers and stepped into the subway car heading to Queens. Of course, there were no empty seats, but then if she'd wanted to sit on the ride home, she should have had that drink with Gwen and Ajay and caught a later train.

"I can walk you home if you want. Make sure you get there safe and sound." Ajay stood next to her. "I'm even willing to hang out on your sofa."

"I'm fine, Ajay. The super changed the locks, and it's been a week with no hassles."

"I can make my famous martinis." He winked. The gesture wasn't as sexy as he imagined.

"Not tonight."

"Okay, then I'll get off at the next stop." He embraced her

before making his way to the door to wait with the crowd exiting the train.

She gripped the pole near the door and spread her feet to keep her balance. Tomorrow was another long day. If it was anything like the last two sessions, then *Beauty Bar* should like her work. Freelance photography wasn't an easy business. Taking pictures and selling them to online retailers didn't pay enough to cover her rent on the warehouse and her apartment. She needed another large client.

Tonight, right after she washed off the subway grime and sweat, she'd start looking for more assignments to book. Why couldn't she get one of those jobs in some exotic place, like Mykonos or Santorini in Greece or the Great Wall of China? As much as she loved living in New York, getting away for the summer would have advantages.

She snapped her head up. Maybe…maybe her contact at *Beauty Bar* could help her get an assignment on their next location shot. For sure, instead of watching reality television tonight, she'd dig around online to see if she could find another dream assignment out of the city. Could she be lucky enough to find something that would allow her to take both Ajay and Gwen?

The train pulled into the Briarwood-Van Wyck Blvd station. She adjusted her bag on her shoulder and exited the car. She couldn't wait to get above ground. Even if the air outside were as hot as before, at least there would be more enjoyable aromas than perspiration, sweat, and hopelessness.

She made her way up the stairs and into the early cast of evening. The sun had dipped behind the high-rises, leaving the sky a combination of light blue and navy. The streets near the subway were busy. The crowds thinned out as she neared her place. She was already changing gears into relax mode. Even though a cool shower called her name, she took her time walking the six blocks to her third-floor walk-up.

The red brick building with the welcoming awning came into view. The tension in her shoulders melted away. The street was quiet. Where were the kids that were supposed to be outside enjoying summer and the joy of no homework?

Before opening the door to the building, she glanced up and down the street. Except for the honking horns a few streets away and the hum of air conditioners, there was no other noise. No one was lurking to overpower her and take her hostage.

Her father wanted her to have a building with a doorman, but he had no idea what an apartment in a building like that cost. She climbed the stairs to her unit. By the time she reached the third floor, the back of her dress was damp again. She made her way down the hall and stopped just outside her apartment to fish the key from her purse.

She put the key in the lock and turned, but the door was already open.

CHAPTER 2

Olivia backed down the hall, almost tripping over her feet while trying to juggle her bags. Her heart rate picked up. Getting as far away from the apartment as she could was the only thing that mattered, right now. She took the stairs two at a time, balancing her purse and the messenger bags on her shoulder. In the lobby, she pulled her phone from her bag and scrolled through the contacts. When she found David's number, she tapped the screen.

"Hey, girl, what's up?" David's voice was chipper just like always.

"My apartment door's unlocked," she whispered, glancing over her shoulder.

David said nothing for several seconds. She heard rustling in the background. "David!" she yelled his name.

"Yeah, I'm here. I was moving to hear you better. I don't understand. Your door's unlocked—why is that important?"

She took a short breath. "I just got home from work. I went to my apartment door. It's already unlocked." Each word came out with a gush of air.

"Are you sure you secured it this morning?"

"Yes. I double- checked it. I always do now."

"Did you go in?"

"No."

"Where are you now?"

"In the lobby. David, I'm scared." She tried to bite back the tears. Nobody liked a hysterical woman.

"I'll be right there. Call 911 and stay put. Give me three minutes. I'm still in my jogging clothes, so I'll run."

Olivia dropped her bags onto the floor and dialed the emergency number. She gave the operator the information, forcing her voice to sound level as she enunciated the address. The last thing she wanted to do was screw up the address and no one show up.

She ended the call and focused on the surveillance camera in the lobby, making sure she was in full view of it as she walked from the door and back. With each loop her heart slowed a little.

Maybe she'd overreacted.

Maybe the super had been in her unit and just forgot to close-up after he left.

Maybe she'd only imagined the door was unlocked.

She stopped at the entrance door and stuck her head out to peer down the street for David. He wasn't in sight yet.

Making friends with someone on the NYPD had been a smart move. And even better, he only lived two blocks away. She added up all the reasons her father may have been right about her living so far from home. Right about her striking out on such an unstable career. Right about her inability to protect herself in a city that never slowed down.

David burst through the double glass doors. There was a slight bulge on his right side below his armpit, his gun.

Thank God he'd brought his gun.

"Are you okay?" he said before he even reached her.

She nodded.

"Did you call the police?"

"Yes."

"They'll be here any minute, then." He put his arm around her.

"Eva doesn't mind you coming over, does she? You guys weren't busy?" Olivia asked.

"No, she doesn't mind. We were getting ready to eat dinner. She wanted to come, too but I told her I didn't think that was a good idea." David was patient and easy to talk to, unlike her brothers who were opinionated and overbearing.

"David, this has to stop. I'm tired of living in fear. There has to be something I can do."

"Don't jump to conclusions. We don't know what's going on yet."

Two uniformed police officers entered the building. The first one was very tall, the other was as thick as the first was tall. Together, they looked like the number ten.

"Hey guys." David pulled his badge from the pocket of his sweatpants and flashed it before shoving it back in place.

"What have we got here?" The taller one spoke first.

"Not sure yet. Olivia says her apartment door was unlocked when she arrived home. She's sure she locked it this morning."

"Did you go in?" The round officer pulled a pad from his pocket.

Olivia forced her tongue to work. "No."

"She's been having issues with a stalker for the past several months. I just got here and told her to call 911," David said. "Let's go upstairs and find out what's going on." David led the way up the three flights of stairs. Olivia followed behind the three men.

"Her place is at the end of the hall. On the left." David pointed. He'd removed his gun and held it at his side in cop mode now.

The tall officer turned to her. "Ma'am, stay here." He pointed to a spot on the carpet.

Olivia froze. She couldn't make her mind process what was going on. One day, life was great, and she was just a happy New Yorker, the next, someone had invaded her life, turning it inside out and upside down and she was helpless. Fighting the things she could see was hard enough, how could she battle a stranger she couldn't even identify?

After several minutes, David stuck his head out the door and waved her down the hall. Walking toward him was like going toward a Halloween Fun House, she wanted to go, but she was afraid to move.

When she reached him, he put his arm around her shoulders. The strain on his face made her breathe harder.

"What is it, David?"

"Someone was here, and it wasn't the super. I'm going to let you go in, but I want you to remain calm. You're not alone, okay?" His words were meant to soothe, but they didn't come close.

"Is someone dead in there?" Her voice wobbled more than her knees.

"No." He rubbed her shoulder before easing her through the door. The strong smell of chemicals filled her nostrils, like the summer her father had sealed their deck and told her to stay off it for two days.

She expelled the air from her lungs, forcing the scent away. The first thing she saw was the kitchen on the left. Everything was the way she'd left it that morning. She was a neat freak. She had to be in the small space or chaos would ensue, especially since her camera equipment seemed to multiply every month.

David nudged her forward. She tilted her head to try and make out what was on the walls. The photographs she took on her trip to Togo and Benin last year were askew. Large red letters covered the living area walls as if they'd been written in a hurry. The writing was hard to make out even though the words were huge and angry. She studied the letters. The words 'YOU BELONG TO ME' written several times on each wall came into focus.

She spun around, counting. That sentence was sprawled on the walls five times. She pressed her palm to her mouth to choke back the noise in her throat. "Is that written in blood?" she croaked.

"No, it's red spray paint. And it's dry which means this happened earlier today."

"Oh, thank God it's not blood." She closed her eyes for a moment. Those words were imprinted on her brain and would remain for a long time. Her body went slack, but she forced herself to stay upright.

"Do you have any idea who might have done this?" the tall officer asked.

"How about my bedroom? Are those walls marked, too?"

"No. It looks like all the damage is right here." The round officer used his pencil to indicate the living room. "It doesn't look like anything else was touched. Just this personal message." He scribbled on his pad. "Does the building have cameras?"

"Yes, in the lobby and on each floor. The last time this happened whoever it was, hid his face from the camera. He knew exactly where the cameras were located," David said.

"The last time?"

"Yes, someone broke in and left three dozen red roses on the kitchen counter." Olivia pointed toward the kitchen.

"Could this be an old boyfriend?" The round officer asked the questions while the tall, thin one strolled around the apartment as if he was already bored.

"This isn't some lover's spat. I don't have any boyfriends. I've dated and believe me, none of them had the time, energy, or inclination to want to get back with me. Whoever is doing this is some jerk, someone who wants to scare the shit out of me. This person is unbalanced."

The two officers came to stand in front of her. The round one pointed to her. "We'll reach out to the super to get the video footage. If you've been down this path before, I don't expect the suspect decided to show his face this time, so don't expect much."

"He? You think it's a man?"

The two officers looked at each other. "Stalkers are usually men and women tend to have men stalkers." The taller one sighed. Giving her this basic information must have been a chore.

"Can't you do something?" She spoke louder than she'd intended.

"We've checked your door. The lock is intact. That means there's no sign of a break-in. so your stalker might have a key."

"I had the lock changed after those flowers showed up on my counter."

"Who has a key to your place?" The officer started scribbling again.

Olivia rubbed her right temple. Her head was thumping as if someone was inside, trying to get out. "Um, the super, of course. And David has one." She nodded toward her him. "My assistants have keys because sometimes they have to stop by here to pick up equipment."

"Your assistants? Could one of them be behind this?"

"No. No." She shook her head—whoever was in it really wanted out now. "They are my friends. They wouldn't do anything like this. Besides, we were together today at a photo shoot in Chelsea." She looked at David. "How could they even ask me such a ridiculous question?"

"Calm down, Olivia," David said. "We'll come up with

something."

"Does anyone else have a key?" The short officer looked bored now too. He was probably upset to have to deal with something as mundane as a stalker. Maybe he would have been happier if there were a dead body on her living room rug and the words had been written in blood.

The look on the officers' faces didn't look nearly as optimistic as David sounded.

"Come down to the station in the morning, and we'll fill out a formal complaint. We need to get something on file." The shorter officer flipped his pad closed and stuffed it into his back pants pocket.

"Don't you want to dust for prints, take some pictures, call in a forensics crew?" Olivia's words rushed out.

David nodded to the officers. It must have been some police code she didn't understand, because without saying anything, both officers walked out of the apartment as if they'd been dismissed.

"Why aren't they doing something, David? Why did you let them go?"

"Olivia, it doesn't work that way. They're not going to pull the forensics team off a major job to dust your apartment for fingerprints. Where's your camera?"

She spun around. "I left my bags in the lobby. Do you think—" She dashed out.

"Where are you going?" David followed her down the hall.

"I've got to get my camera bag. Suppose someone steals it? I'm still paying for that equipment." She ran down the stairs, her heart beating faster than her feet were moving. This day couldn't get any worse.

Her shoes hit the lobby floor with a smack. Her bag was still in the same place. With a deep breath, she pushed the strap of her dress back onto her shoulder and headed back upstairs.

One. Two. Three. Four. Five. Counting calmed her. She might have to get to eighty before she felt the effect.

David stood on the third-floor landing. "Olivia," he said her name like he was getting ready to give her a lecture. "You have got to slow down. I know this has you rattled, but let's take a moment and think about what our next steps will be. Maybe it's time to bring in the Cyber Crimes unit."

"Our next steps? David, nobody is invading your life, making you afraid to go into your own home. I've given up my Facebook account, my Twitter account, and my Snapchat account because this sicko hacked them. I'm afraid to answer my phone. I walk the streets looking over my shoulder. What's going on here isn't an 'our' thing, this is a 'me' thing. And I don't know what I'm going to do."

At the entrance to her apartment, she stopped. The place that had always welcomed her was now the last place she wanted to be. "I don't want to go back in there, David."

"What *do* you want to do?"

She tucked her bottom lip between her teeth. "It was my idea to move to New York. I wanted to prove to my family that I am a grown up. I didn't want to be treated like a little sister any longer." She stood up straighter. "I can't go back to Philly."

"Tell you what. Stay with Eva and me tonight. Together we'll sit down and come up with a plan."

For several moments she said nothing. Her mind was racing through possibilities and alternatives. No matter what happened tonight, she wasn't going to cry. If she wanted everyone to see her as an adult, she had to act like one. "Okay. That's a good idea. Let me go inside and get a few things. I want to take some pictures of my place, too."

"Do you want me to go with you?"

"No. I can do this. I need to do this."

CHAPTER 3

Olivia strolled from the window overlooking the street to the renovated kitchen in the apartment David shared with Eva. The walk wasn't long enough to erase the anxiety in her chest, so she continued the loop again and again. It's funny what you notice when you're not paying attention. The hardwood floors in the living area were darker and thinner-planked than the hardwood floor in the kitchen. Probably another of David's effort to save money

She took several deep breaths, trying to regulate her breathing, get it back to normal—if anything in her life could ever be normal again. Knowing someone had been in her place scribbling on the walls would be with her for a long time. What would have happened if she'd come home while he was in there? A cold shiver claimed her body.

David and Eva's place was two times larger than her one-bedroom unit. The modern decor didn't have the homey feel of her place, but the clean lines and geometric patterns were soothing. Everything here was new and sparkly and shiny. Her home, on the other hand, was furnished with pieces she liked to call vintage instead of second-hand. The pictures that filled her walls had been taken during her many trips to Africa, London, Hong Kong, and Brazil.

Eva came into the room carrying a cup of tea. She had been Olivia's friend first. They still laughed about thet blind date with David that turned out to be love at first sight. Olivia didn't believe in falling in love so quickly, but once in a blue moon, maybe it did happen. At least, that's what happened for David and Eva.

Eva handed her the cup before sitting beside her. "How you doin' sweetie?"

Olivia accepted the cup and stared into the dark brew. "I don't know. I'm numb. My head has been throbbing since I put the key in the lock."

"Let me get you something stronger." Eva stood.

"Not right now. Maybe later." Olivia patted the sofa. "Please just sit with me for now." Olivia stuck her hand into her coiled hair. She had hair like her mother's—thick, full, and hard to manage. Tugging at her curls soothed her like nothing else could lately.

"You know you can stay here as long as you want."

"Eva, I know what you're saying, and I thank you for that. I have a mess—my life is a mess right now. I might not know what I'm going to do this minute, but I've got to do something."

David came back into the room. He'd changed out of his sweats into another pair that was a shade lighter. He flopped into the chair in front of her. "I'll go with you to the station in the morning, but don't get your expectations up."

"I can move again. But what if the stalker finds me? I can't spend the rest of my life running. I shouldn't have to."

David reached for her hands and held them tight. At least he stopped the shaking for a moment. "While I was showering I had an idea."

Olivia leaned in. "I could use a good one of those."

"I don't know if I'd call it that, but hear me out." He paused. She knew him well enough to know his brain was turning over rocks, looking for answers to her problems. "The police aren't going to push your case to the front of their pile. Not because they don't want to, but because they have more serious stuff going on."

"I know, murders, kidnappings, assaults, stuff like that, but I need help, too. I pay taxes. I deserve some attention. And I deserve to come and go as I please. To be safe in my own home."

He squeezed her hand. "I know, and you're right. But above everything else, your safety comes first. I think you should go away for a while. Not forever, maybe a few days— a week tops. While you're gone, and I know you're safe, I'll do some digging around."

Olivia absorbed David's words. Sorted them out and directed there meaning. "Run?"

"No. Just take a break for a week."

"You want me to go away?" She shook her head. "I'm supposed to let this...this sicko run me out of not only my home but the city too?" She jumped up, but she was too exhausted to resume pacing.

"Sit down, Olivia and hear me out. Please."

She returned to the sofa.

"I'll do everything I can to find out who is doing this to you. Even if I have to do it on my own time."

"I can't ask you to do that, David."

"I don't think you're going to be able to stop him, Olivia," said Eva. "You know how he is when he gets something in his head."

"But where would I go? I won't go running home to my parents. And I've got work to do. I have a job coming up for a start-up multi-media company."

"I haven't figured all that out yet, but..."

Olivia flopped back against the cushions. "You know, Ajay asked me about taking a vacation this morning. Maybe this is the perfect time to let him and Gwen have some time off." Olivia warmed to the idea. "I could go to Sebastian Island. I haven't been there in years. I used to go every year with my grandparents, but that was..." She shook her head. "Wow. That was back when I was in junior high. I used to have so much fun down there playing with my sister and brothers."

"Okay, that would work. How soon do you think you could leave?"

Olivia curled a lock of hair around her finger. Could she do this? Could she do this now? "A day or two. What do you think?" She looked at Eva for confirmation.

"I think that's a good idea. Do you think you'll be okay by yourself?" Eva asked.

"Sebastian's a beautiful place. It's the kind of place where you can leave your keys in the car overnight. Where you don't have to lock up everything with a deadbolt. Everyone knows everyone else. It would be the perfect place." The idea took root in her head. "You know, with a little luck I can take some pictures of the tranquility for my client to sell them on the idea of shooting their ads there. So, for me, it could be a little bit of work and a little bit of pleasure." She nodded. "I'll call Gwen tonight and ask her to make the arrangements for me."

David put up his hand. "No. I don't want you to tell anyone where you're going."

She looked at David, then over to Eva. "But why? You don't think—"

"No, I don't. I really don't. But let me do some snooping around before we tell anyone where you are. Eva can help you make the arrangements tonight and tomorrow. For now, I want to keep this between us."

"David, I have a favor to ask you." Olivia stared at David's face.

He rubbed his hands together. He was always ready to help. "What is it?"

"I want you to help me pick out a gun."

"Olivia, slow down. You don't know anything about guns."

"I grew up with two brothers and a father who went deer hunting every season. I've even gone to the range with my family. I know I haven't held or used a gun in a long time, but I'm hoping it's like riding a bicycle and my muscle memory will kick in."

He exhaled. Even before he opened his mouth, Olivia heard his objection. "Can you wait until you come back? You won't need a gun in Sebastian. If you think you need something to protect yourself, I'll get you pepper spray tomorrow to take with you."

She nodded. The three of them were quiet for several seconds. The suggestion had an upside; a whole week without worrying what was going to happen next. She started mentally packing.

CHAPTER 4

*X*ander Fitzgerald kept his focus on the tarmac as the plane taxied toward the gate. Sitting in the first-class lounge with the free-flowing wine did not make up for all the time wasted while waiting for a crew member to show up. The delay at JFK almost guaranteed he'd be late for the conference call this afternoon. He ticked off the tasks he could have accomplished if the flight had arrived as scheduled.

He took this flight once a month, so he knew what was going to happen next. He waited for the captain to come over the intercom with the instructions that Xander knew verbatim.

Almost on cue, the crackle of the intercom filled the cabin.

"Folks, please remain seated until the seatbelt light is turned off. We're just waiting on the stairs to be brought over, then we'll start deplaning. Enjoy your stay on Sebastian Island."

If Xander rushed, he might make it home instead of having to make the call from his cell in the car. The projects were piling up. He'd have to find a way to weed some of them out. While everyone wanted his protection expertise, he only worked for reputable clients with deep pockets and something worth preserving. Only those on the right side of the law.

The moment the seatbelt light went off, he stood. He pulled his overnight bag from under the seat, then exited the plane. The advantage of being over six feet tall was it allowed him to walk faster than the average slow-moving tourist who only wanted to take their time and enjoy the island.

He'd moved to Sebastian Island to get away from the hectic pace of D.C. And from Hope. Ironically, as it turned out, their relationship was hopeless as well. She broke things off with him because he wouldn't commit. Here on Sebastian, the chances of running into her were nil, and that's what he wanted. He needed the peace the island provided. Life on the island was slower for some, but not for him. He needed his work to keep his mind from wandering from one woman to the next. According to his mother, it was time for him to settle down. While the idea sounded like a good one, settling down with one woman wasn't wired into his DNA. That was something his mother needed to accept.

He stopped at the escalator and glanced at his watch. There was no way he would make it home in time. With a deep sigh, he hopped onto the moving stairs. His notes were on his desk. He envisioned the folder on the corner. The only thing he could do now was try to delay the call or wing it from memory. He'd take his chance. Maybe—with just a little luck—the car would already be waiting outside to take him home.

The unclouded sky on the island didn't change much. It was one of the best things about living here. The heat sizzled everything. He loved the consistency of the weather. It was dependable. He didn't like change, interruption or delays. It was one of those idiosyncrasies that he'd gotten used to about himself; as long as things stayed the same he was a happy man.

He made his way to the car line. There was only one black sedan at the curb, in the usual spot where his island driver waited for him to return from his monthly trip to the States.

Another glance at his watch told him he was going to be late. Making adjustments to the plan on the fly opened the door for something to go wrong. A missed contract detail or a miscommunication of scope, but today there was no choice. He had to try and delay his conference call with Jacob until he reached home. He wanted to have the specifics in front of him before they talked. Xander pulled his cell from his pocket and dialed.

"Jacob, I'm glad I was able to reach you. I just landed. I wanted you to know I might be late for our call. Can we push it back thirty minutes?"

The other end of the phone was quiet longer than Xander wanted. Jacob wanted to play hardball—exercise his authority or flex his pseudo-authority. Xander had enough patience to wait as long as it took.

"That's not going to work. I've got a full day. We had an appointment, and I rearranged my day to talk with you at eleven. Find a way to make it work," Jacob demanded.

"How about later today? I can call you as late as you like. Or we can talk now that I've got you on the line. We're only talking about a ten-minute difference." Negotiating with Jacob was impossible, but he had to give it a try.

"No. Won't work. It's got to be at eleven. I've got some-thing going on now."

"Okay. I'll call you at eleven." Xander stomped his foot. Jacob was a prick, no doubt about it.

"I know you will." Jacob disconnected the call.

Xander examined the dark screen for several moments

before placing it back in his pocket. Working with Jacob would be impossible. The man was rigid, demanding and authoritarian, all qualities that meant he was going to shred Xander's good nature. If Jacob wasn't willing to be flexible now, then what was going to happen when Xander had real challenges for him?

He made his way to the sedan and climbed into the back seat.

OLIVIA COLLECTED HER LUGGAGE, then followed the signs to the car service area. Outside the terminal, the humidity enveloped her like it had been waiting for her to show up and welcome her to the island. Maybe it was the relief of being away or the idea of taking this vacation, but something buoyed her steps. The muggy weather wasn't oppressive enough to erase the joy brightening her mood.

The need to stick her freshly pedicured toes into the turquoise water ratcheted up. With Eva's help, she'd found a small house to rent. The description said it was just a few feet from the water with expansive ocean views. Relaxation awaited just minutes away.

She spotted the car area and rushed forward. The paper Eva had given her had the house address and confirmation number for the car. Before she reached the idling black sedan, a man climbed inside.

As she approached the car, she checked the license plate against the paper in her hand again before sticking her head inside the vehicle. "What are you doing in my car?"

"I'm sorry, this is my car." At least he didn't sound as testy as she felt.

She pulled off her sunglasses to get a better look at the information. "I'm sorry, there must be some mistake. I'm looking at my documentation, and I've got the right car. Can you show me your paperwork?" she said.

"I don't have any. I do this every month." He slid across the seat and out of the car. He was at least a foot taller than she, and lean, with just enough stubble on his face to give him a distinguished look. His short dark hair and thick brow were in sharp contrast to his ivory complexion. "I'm really in a hurry. Is there any way you can make arrangements with another car?"

"I—uh—I ..." Olivia looked around. A string of taxis was a short walk away. The line waiting for them was even longer. "No. No, I won't. This is my car. I made the arrangements, and I'm going to enjoy that air conditioning from here until I get to my rental."

He waved a gentleman over who had to be the driver of the car. Olivia struggled to keep her anger in check. Some unknown person had her fleeing New York, and now another man wanted to push her aside and take her car. Was there a note on her back that said 'sucker'?

Olivia held her paper out to the suited driver. "This is my car. I've got the paperwork right here. Can you please tell this gentleman to get his stuff and get out of my car? I'm going to this address right here." She pointed to the top of the document.

The driver scanned the sheet, then pulled a folded piece of paper from his pocket. He unfolded it and ran his finger down the crease before turning to the intruder. "I'm sorry, Mr. Fitzgerald. She's right. Today, this is her car. I never even checked my paperwork before leaving the terminal." He nodded his head toward her but kept his eyes on Xander. "Did you book a car this month?"

"I thought I did." Mr. Fitzgerald rubbed his chin." How soon can you get another car here?"

The driver's eyes enlarged. "I can have a car here in less than an hour."

"Agh! That's not going to work." He looked over her head at the taxi stand.

"May I make a suggestion?" the driver said. "You both are going in the same direction. Mr. Fitzgerald is on the hill, and you're just below him on the beach. I can drop him off and take you straight to your place." His luminous smile against his brown skin was almost enough to convince her.

"I'll pay for the entire ride if you'll agree," Mr. Fitzgerald offered.

Olivia sighed. To refuse his suggestion would make her sound like a bitch. To accept would make her a push-over. She was more comfortable being a push-over when she didn't have to pay for it. "I guess that's okay." She climbed into the backseat, then Mr. Fitzgerald climbed in beside her.

"Aren't you going to sit in the front seat?"

"I would, but he has his stuff cluttering the seat. I'm sorry for the inconvenience. I go to the States once a month, and when I return my car is waiting. I assumed—, incorrectly, that this was my car." The sincerity in his voice was enough to soften her anger.

She stuck out her hand. "I'm Olivia. I'm glad we were able to work something out."

He didn't exactly smile, but his greenish-blue eyes twinkled enough to let her know her earlier attitude hadn't angered him. "I'm Xander Fitzgerald. If your place is at the bottom of the hill, you must be staying in the Macklemore house. That place has some wonderful views."

"That's what the website says. I'm looking forward to a quiet, relaxing vacation." She kept her voice professional, using the no-nonsense technique she'd developed in the world of men and photography. No matter how good-looking he was, this was not the time to notice. She had one nutjob in her life she needed to get rid of, she didn't need to invite another stranger into her life. She wanted to be left alone. Being here was only a visit—a moment to get away from her real-life issues, not a time to start new ones.

"Was that a hint to let me know you don't want me to come down the hill and enjoy the view from your porches?"

"I'm not trying to be rude. I'm leaving a situation back home, and my sole goal while I'm here is to get away. I won't be doing any entertaining. Sorry."

"Got it." He gave her a quick thumbs-up. "I need to make a call. I hope you don't mind. I'll stay on my side of the car and won't bother you again." He gave her his back, shutting her out.

CHAPTER 5

*X*ander strolled onto his balcony. The sun had settled low on the horizon, his favorite time of day when he shut down the work part of his life and enjoyed the frills. Even though there was no one in his life to share his toys with, he managed. He settled into the Adirondack chair overlooking the ocean, placing his feet on the rail and took a long swallow from the glass of brandy.

The call with Jacob hadn't gone well. Like most men used to being in charge, Jacob wasn't pleased to hear they wouldn't be doing business together. It didn't take much research to find out that Jacob's business interests weren't all legal. The moment Jacob thought he could bully Xander into protecting his warehouses and the shady transactions was the moment to cut ties.

Xander swirled the Bourbon in his glass before draining the remaining contents. The Macklemore house was lit up. Almost every room in the house had the warm glow of incandescent lights. Perched on the side of the hill, his view of the sunset was much better than Olivia Sika's, the photographer from Queens, New York. Yes, he'd done some research. Part of his search was professional reasons. He liked knowing who his neighbors were, and the other part was all carnal. She'd torched his animal instinct. Her exotic beauty had captured him the moment she'd stuck her head into the car. He'd wanted to know more about the dark, beautiful Olivia with the African flair. He suppressed a smile. She hadn't fallen for his charm—which meant he needed to sharpen his skills. He didn't get much practice on the island.

As if he'd summoned her, she stepped out onto her porch. Her ebony skin and the gold cuffs around her wrists glowed in the waning sunlight. She had pulled her hair back into a giant curly puff at the nape of her neck. He sat up to get a better look at his new temporary neighbor. Her bright, vibrant African print bikini would leave a lasting impression on his mind. Seeing her in those tiny pieces of material would fuel his dreams tonight.

Her movements were fluid, like those of a trained ballerina. She glided across the deck like electricity in motion. The energy pouring out of her was almost infectious. He should have looked away, giving her some privacy, but he couldn't. The long, smooth column of her neck allowed her large hoop earrings to dangle just above her shoulders.

She went inside but came back out within seconds. With a hefty camera in her hand, she adjusted the lens and snapped pictures of the sunset. Her smooth moves were as mesmerizing as the bestselling thriller waiting for him on his nightstand.

The way she handled the camera said she knew what she was doing. No cell phone photos for this beautiful woman who captured his imagination like no one had in a long time. She handled the camera the same way he handled his tools. She disappeared from view for a moment. He stood, not ready for the show to be over yet. If she hadn't made her position so clear, he would have dropped by with a welcome to the neighborhood gift—and he didn't mean the boner in his britches.

She appeared on the other side of the circular porch, snapping pictures of the wild hibiscus growing on the hillside. She had to be the most fascinating person to rent the house since he'd lived here. She continued her way around the porch, adjusting her lens every few seconds, until she swung around, pointing her camera at his house.

He couldn't be sure she focused on him, but he waved. From the way she dropped the camera and marched inside, she must have seen him.

The ping of his cell phone captured his attention. Since the show was over for the night, he raced inside to answer it. The only person who dared interrupt him this time of evening was his mother or sister. He reached for his cell on his desk. Jacob's number appeared on the screen. He hadn't gotten around to blocking his calls yet.

He answered. "Jacob, I made my position very clear."

"I wanted to give you an opportunity to reconsider. I'm offering you an opportunity to make millions of dollars on my New York business alone. You're the best at what you do, and I want you on my team."

"I'm not interested, Jacob." Talking to the slime on the phone was more than he wanted to do.

"What can I do to get you to change your mind?"

"Jacob, you don't know me very well. I'm not the kind of man who changes his mind." He ended the call.

CHAPTER 6

Once inside the house, Olivia flipped the lock, then double-checked to ensure it was secure. How long had he been spying on her? He could have been watching her all afternoon. He wasn't her stalker, but he made her as uncomfortable as the real one back in New York.

She rushed around the house closing every shutter on the back of the house. If he wanted to observe her, she wasn't going to give him a clear shot.

In the master bedroom that faced the ocean, she turned on the small flat-screen television positioned on the dresser to watch the news. According to the newscaster, there was a festival going on this weekend, and everyone was supposed to wear a straw hat. A car chase last night that led the police through a family neighborhood ended when the shoplifter gave up. The weather was going to be hot and humid, and a hurricane forming off the coast of Africa was projected to move toward the Atlantic Ocean. The forecast was uncertain of the exact track but warned Sebastian residents to prepare just in case. She turned off the television and fell back onto the bed. Bad luck had attached to the bottom of her shoe, and nothing was going to shake it loose.

Now was an excellent time to find out who Xander Fitzgerald was. If he could spy on her from his house, she needed to do a little investigating of her own. She turned on her computer and waited for the screen to come to life. She typed his name into the search field. There were several images of people named Xander Fitzgerald, but none of them looked like the handsome man in the house on the hill. A quick check of the social media links didn't provide any details, either. She tapped her fingers against the keys. There was good reason for her to be absent on social media— thanks to her stalker—but why was he?

She'd let David talk her into giving up her social media accounts. According to him, her posts were like telephoning her stalker with information about her life. Not only had the decision hindered her ability to get work, but she also had nothing to do to waste away time.

She dialed David's number to catch him before his evening run. If she had to stay off social media, he could at least hear her gripe about it. "I'm here. I've unpacked. I'm bored."

"Good. Don't you feel better already? Safe?"

"I feel like I ran away. I understand why you thought this was best for me, but in a week, I'm coming home regardless of what you've found out. I'll buy a gun and get proficient at using it. But I won't keep hiding. And no more running."

"Okay. That means I have a week to find out what's going on," he said. "I spoke to someone in cyber-crimes. They might be willing to look at your case, but like everything else they're understaffed. I'll try to lean on them."

"That's the best news I've heard in a while."

"Don't get excited yet. What do you have planned while you're there?"

"Take pictures, consume drinks with little umbrellas in them, and sit on the beach...oh yeah. There is a very handsome man who lives behind my place, and I plan to avoid him."

"Good idea. I don't think you should trust anyone. Not until we know more."

"Tell me this is all temporary. Tell me my life is going to get back to normal."

"That's my plan. I'll do everything I can."

"I've got my pepper spray on my nightstand." She glanced over her shoulder at her secret weapon.

"Remember, the idea is to disable someone so you can get away. Nothing more."

"Yeah, you don't have to remind me."

She ended the call. There was one more thing she had to do before going to bed. She made another sweep of the house, making sure everything was locked and closed. Her behavior was overkill, but she wouldn't be able to fall asleep until her rampant worry settled down.

After all the travel, she should have been exhausted, but her body would not cooperate. In the darkened room, she reached for her tablet. A little reading usually helped her fall asleep. She fluffed the pillows behind her and leaned into the comfort. When her eyelids grew heavy, the words on the page faded to nothing.

Olivia was startled awake. Something thumped outside. Or was that her imagination? She couldn't be sure where the sound came from or if the noise was some leftover residual from New York still lingering in her subconscious. The room was dark—dark enough to paralyze her in the bed. From the sliding glass door, a hint of moonlight filtered through the curtains. Her heart pounded against her ribs, a feeling that had become too familiar.

She patted the nightstand until her hand landed on the

recognizable feel of the pepper spray. If she weren't such a chicken, she would have ventured beyond the bedroom, but there was only so much pepper spray could do to protect her.

There was no way her stalker could have followed her here. This was her life, not some horror movie on late night television. She was afraid to move—jumping at every sound. Even the low roar of the ocean in the distance didn't sound as friendly and welcoming as it had earlier.

By the time the sun lit up the sky, she could count the hours of sleep she'd gotten on three fingers. A constant check of her phone through the night and she'd seen two o'clock, three-thirty and four-fifty-five. Exhaustion and sleeplessness clouded her head, but she swung her legs off the bed anyway. How much of what had happened last night was real and how much was her overactive imagination, she couldn't tell.

At the bedroom sliding glass doors, she pulled back the curtains to stare at the ocean. One of the joys of being so close to the water's edge was seeing the sunrise. In Queens, she never saw the sun come up. By the time she exited the apartment in the morning, the sun was already cresting the skyscrapers.

Olivia was in her swimsuit and sarong within minutes. Even without a good night's sleep, she had the energy to sightsee all day. Seeing her first sunrise in years was the way to start.

On the beach, she pushed her toes into the sand. She pulled her camera from the bag. The day was going to be warm and sunny, but for now, the gentle breeze pushed her hair across her face and the camera lens.

A noise behind her made her jump up. With the pepper spray in her right hand, she grabbed a handful of sand with her other hand and flung it.

"Hey, what's up with you?" Xander jumped back, using the towel in his hand to wipe his face.

"Why would you sneak up on me like that? What the hell is wrong with you?"

His eyes narrowed. "I came down for a swim. I do every morning. Just in case you thought the beach belonged only to you, let me inform you that it does not. I had no idea you were even here."

"So, you weren't spying like last night?"

He strolled closer to her. She backed up. "Last night I was on my deck, minding my own business when you took my picture without asking my permission."

"Look, I had no idea this beach was public." She waved her arm to the water. "Please, go ahead. I'm sorry about the sand, but you startled me."

"Apology accepted. I'm sorry I scared you. I usually take my morning swim without an audience." He dropped his towel and sauntered into the water. Nobody walked that sexily, that athletically, that sinewy, unless he was trying to get her attention. The muscles in his thighs looked like massive missiles. There wasn't a part of his body that didn't sport a muscle. She was a photographer, so handsome men weren't new to her, but Xander wasn't just good-looking. He was a man with attitude. A lot of attitude.

He disappeared into the strong waves within seconds. She lifted the camera and reset the shutter speed to capture his smooth strokes as he sliced the water. His head popped up every few minutes as he swam across the horizon.

The sun had made its full appearance by the time Xander climbed out of the ocean. He walked toward her. Water dripped from his hair and his body. He sat down beside her without waiting for an invitation.

While he ran the towel through his dark hair, she studied him. His arms were as impressive as his legs. She could only imagine what it would feel like pressed against his rippled chest.

"I meant it when I said I was sorry. I should have tried to make more noise as I came down the hill. Next time I'll kick pebbles or whistle or something."

"Okay. And I promise not to throw sand or anything else at you." She tucked her camera back into the bag.

"Tell me why such a beautiful woman is vacationing alone on our beautiful island," he said.

"How do you know I'm alone?" She could hear David in her ear telling her to be careful.

"I'd have to be a moron if I didn't notice just the two of us rode here in the car. Last night you were outside by yourself and again this morning..." He looked over her shoulder. "You're alone."

"I didn't see anyone with you on your deck last night."

"That you didn't. I live alone in the house up the hill, and I'm not ashamed to say it."

"I'm not ashamed either, but I don't think my circumstances are any of your business."

"Typical remark for someone from the States."

"Screw you." Why was she letting this man get to her?

"Not now. Maybe later. I'll check my schedule."

"Are you always this straightforward?"

"Always."

For a moment they were quiet, each staring out at the water.

"What are you doing today?" He had a natural smile that put her at ease.

"Has anyone ever told you that you're nosy?"

"There is a difference between asking questions and being nosey. I have a natural curiosity."

She nodded slowly, studying his mannerisms a little at a time. His easy smile, his dark brown hair, the scuff on his chin, his toned body...he wasn't the average guy, for sure. "As you can see, I'm a photographer. I'm going to the lavender farm to take lots of pictures."

"I hope you're not planning to go to the Clawson farm. It closed a few years ago."

She removed the band from her hair, allowing her curls to fall free. "I didn't know."

"The Randall Farm is even bigger. It's not too far. I can show you where it is."

"Oh, you don't have to do that. I was going to ride one of the bikes. You know, ride around, stopping wherever I want. I might even take a picture of a fruit fly today."

"That sounds like fun. I'd love to join you, and I actually have a bike. I promise to be the perfect tour guide. What do you say?"

"This isn't a date or anything like that is it?"

"I wouldn't dare try to date you without telling you." He made a rough gesture of crossing his heart that would have shamed anyone who was Catholic. "What time should I expect you to pick me up?" He smiled again. "I mean, since you have to come up the hill, you might as well stop by my house."

She pushed the camera strap onto her shoulder, then stood. "I'm going to shower and change. Give me an hour."

"You don't need to change," he mumbled into his hand, but she heard him anyway.

She quickened her steps across the sand to her place. A quick glance over her shoulder had her locking eyes with Xander. His fierce gaze warmed her flesh.

CHAPTER 7

Xander kept his eyes on Olivia until she disappeared into her house. Her small footprints pressed in the sand beckoned him to follow, but this wasn't the time, she'd been clear about her intentions. He shook his head like a wet dog.

He was going to blow off all his business calls and spend the day with a woman that was so attractive he couldn't stop thinking about her. Even though she held him in contempt— and maybe she should—somehow, he was going to change her mind. Beauties like that didn't come into his life every day.

He wrapped the towel around his waist. By the time he reached his place, he had mapped out the whole day for the two of them. His cell phone rang. Instead of answering, he rushed to the shower. Olivia didn't look like the kind of woman to keep waiting.

Olivia was outside his door in less than an hour. Her camera bag perched in the basket on the front of her bike.

"Shall we go?" He pointed to his bike that he'd pulled from the small storage shed behind the house. "Since you don't go anywhere without your camera, I can tell you're a photographer. What else can you tell me about yourself?"

"You already know more about me than I know about you. Why don't you tell me your life's story?" She mounted her bike and started to pedal. "You haven't always lived in this house. I remember coming here as a young girl and the family that owned this house were island natives. Their skin was darker than mine," she called over her shoulder.

He climbed onto his bike and caught up with her. They rode side-by-side. "Do you always say what's on your mind?"

"Always."

"I bought this house three years ago when I moved here from Washington, D.C."

"What do you do for a living?"

"You'd rather ask questions than answer them, I see."

"Let's say I'm a better listener than I am a talker."

"In my line of work, people who listen more than they talk tend to have something to hide," he said.

She pedaled faster as if she was trying to make talking harder.

"You haven't told me your line of work yet." Her curly hair blew across her face.

"I'm in the protection and security business."

"What does that mean? Are you a security guard or Secret Service?"

"We'll need to turn left at the next intersection. The lavender farm is less than a mile down this road." He pulled ahead of her, not allowing her to catch up. She wasn't the only one who didn't want to talk about some things.

At the entrance, they both stopped, and Olivia took several pictures of the old wooden sign with 'Randal Farms' in large purple lettering. Then she turned the camera on him and snapped several times before he could turn away.

"Don't you just love that smell?" She inhaled.

"I never paid any attention to this place, so I can pretend to like the smell or, I can be truthful and say I'm just your tour guide today. The lavender doesn't smell as good as you do."

"You don't need to flatter me. I know you're lying because all I did was shower. I smell like soap." Her voice rose at the end of the sentence, and the way she cut her eyes at him was a clear indication she wasn't falling for his charm. He climbed off his bike. Together they walked toward the small hut to pay the entrance fee.

When she placed her camera to her eye, she could have been in another time zone. She grunted at his questions when she bothered to answer him at all. He could have been one of the willowy plants for as much attention as she showed him.

After an hour, she must have remembered he was following her around. She turned to him. "What else is there to see? Is there something else near here?"

He pointed over his shoulder toward the entrance. "I'm going to head home. You're fine without my help." He knew when a woman wasn't interested. He'd been involved with a few, and things didn't tend to get better over time.

They locked eyes. She dropped her head. Halfway back to the hut, she grabbed his arm. "I'm being a jerk to you, and I'm sorry. Let me treat you to lunch."

"Why? Do you want to spend a little more time with me because you aren't done ignoring me yet?" His tone was light enough that she should have heard the humor in his voice.

"I deserved that. How about it?" She still held on to his arm.

"Sure. There's a nice sandwich shop nearby. They have a conch soup that's the best in the Caribbean."

She studied his eyes. Instead of looking away, he held her gaze. He was amazed at the intensity of his attraction to her.

But there was no way he'd let her know just how much she was impacting him. He wasn't a school-boy and he didn't believe in instant attraction. What was going on in his chest was all about hormones *and* his overactive libido *and* his vivid imagination *and* his desire to touch her velvety skin.

$\mathcal{S}$eated across the table from Xander at the sandwich shop wasn't a bad deal. The smell of homemade bread made Olivia hungry. For a man, Xander was very chatty, asking more questions than he answered. Like her, he wasn't revealing much. She should have come to Sebastian under an alias.

After placing their lunch order, she observed him like she did everything and everyone, studying his facial angles, where the light hit his cheekbones and the point on his chin, the way his smile grew in intensity until his eyes turned into tiny slits.

He reminded her of her father and brothers. Solid. Self-assured. Strong enough for a woman like her. If only there were a way to clone him and take the replica back to New York, life could be perfect. She wanted a man in her life, but the guys she came across complained about her long work days or the male models she spent so much time with or her need for independence.

"You're staring at me," said Xander.

"It's a habit." She shook her head. "When I have a camera

to my face I can look at almost anything for as long as I want. I can stare without anyone knowing or feeling uncomfortable. My work carries over into my private life."

"Did you stare at me before taking my picture last night?"

"Let me go on the record and say I always stare." She pulled her camera from the bag, slid off the long lens and replaced it with a shorter one. With her elbows on the table, she brought his face into focus and snapped several times. Xander was good- looking, but far from conceited. His manners were impeccable, and even if she had no intention of keeping these pictures now, she had a reason to stare as long as she wanted.

He put his hand over the lens. "That's enough. I'm at a disadvantage. You're using that thing as a weapon. How would you feel if I took out my phone and began taking your picture?"

"Good point. I like being behind the camera, but not in front of one." She shoved the camera back into the bag. "Let's have a drink. I want one that comes with an umbrella." She scanned the menu.

"Do you care what's in the drink?"

"Nope. I got so little sleep last night, the only thing I want to do right now is eat lunch, then go home and take a nap."

"Jet lag?"

"No. I wish. I think it's the island noises I'm not used to. Give me honking horns and sirens, and I can sleep. But here, it's so quiet. I can hear every night bird and tree frog."

"I sleep with my window open and let the sound of the ocean lull me to sleep. Give it a try."

"Yeah, right. Like that's going to happen." She hadn't slept with an open window in months and she wasn't about to now. That would be akin to inviting her stalker into her bedroom to, serve up his terror first class.

The server arrived with their lunch. By the time she

finished her sandwich and drink, she was better, filled with a new burst of energy.

"I noticed a little shop on our way to the restaurant. Do you think I can check it out before heading back?"

"Yes, let's do that." He stood and dropped several bills on the table.

"This is my treat." She handed him the money.

"I owe you for letting me share the car. I insist." He took the bill and put them back.

They made their way to the artsy shop. Xander hung back while she cruised up and down the aisles. She spotted the solid brass carving of an African warrior and smiled. It matched the one she'd picked up in Benin during her visit. She waved the salesperson over. "What can you tell me about this carving?"

The salesperson held the hefty statue in her hand. "This was carved by a local artist. He's from Africa and often makes pieces for us."

"Do you know where in Africa he's from?"

She shook her head. "I don't. But he usually comes in on Wednesday morning. Why don't you stop back in and you can talk to him yourself? I'm sure he'd be honored."

Olivia nodded. "I will. But for now, I'll take this piece."

She paid for the purchase. While the salesperson wrapped the statue in tissue paper, she studied Xander who had his back turned. So far, the day was one of the best she'd had in too long to remember. She'd taken pictures for pure pleasure, something she hadn't done in months. She'd spent the day with a handsome man, which was enjoyable. Her life had been on hold for so long she didn't know how to advance the frame. And until she found out who was trying to ruin her life, she couldn't start a new one.

At the door, she held the colorfully printed bag up for Xander to see. "I bought myself something pretty. And, if I'm right, a gentleman from Benin is the artist. It looks like the artwork I saw when I was there."

"What's significant about Benin?"

"My great-great grandparents were from there. I took a trip there last year, tracing my genealogy."

He nodded several times. "I keep saying I'm going to do that one day. I just haven't found the time."

She mounted her bike. "Ready to head back?" Without waiting for him to reply, she pedaled away. Within a few yards, he pulled ahead of her, not by much, but enough to keep his dignity intact. "Men!" she yelled at him.

They rode single file until the road widened enough for her to pull alongside him. It wasn't long before he was ahead of her again. Her legs were fatigued. The wind against her skin was hot and sticky no matter how fast she peddled. The feeling of being free made her pedal faster. She'd never done anything like this in New York. It wasn't just being away from the stalker, but being outside in the sun, the smell of the ocean and, of course, having Xander's attention for most of the day.

The sound of the car behind them would have gone unnoticed, but the engine revved up. The guardrail gave her nowhere to go. She pedaled faster. In a few feet, she could pull over onto the grassy side of the road. In an instant, the paranoia was back. If something didn't look right, or smell right or sound right, her instincts said get out of the way.

The car revved again. She inched over as much as she could, but access to the shoulders seemed to get farther away. "Why won't he go around?" she yelled to Xander.

"Just ignore him. We have the right of way." He seemed unperturbed.

In a flash, the car clipped the rear wheel of her bicycle. She was airborne for what seemed like hours. There was nothing to grab onto, to anchor her. The only thing she had time to do was scream before she went over the guardrail. She hit the ground with a thud that sounded like it broke all her bones. As hot as it was, the grass and underbrush felt cool, scratching her skin as she tumbled to a stop in a ditch a few feet from the road.

CHAPTER 9

*T*he sound of Olivia's scream echoed in Xander's ears, but before he could glance over his shoulder, the car rammed his bike off the road. He slid across the grass and landed on the soft turf on the side of the road. The dark sedan sped off, accelerating so fast he only got a quick glance at the license plate. XJK. He scrambled to his feet, taking note of the dark color, and the rental car sticker pasted on the bumper.

"Olivia!" He yelled her name as he made his way to where her bike basket sat in the middle of the road. "Olivia, can you hear me?" He spotted the crumpled bike before he saw her yellow shorts and long legs. At least she was sitting up.

He hopped over the rail and made his way down the embankment. "Are you okay?" He checked her over, examining for protruding bones or open gashes, but there were only a few superficial cuts on her legs.

"I don't think I broke anything if that's what you mean." She brushed grass off her shoulder. The pained look on her face said she wasn't okay.

"It's all right, Olivia." He kneeled to embrace her. "Just a native in a hurry to go nowhere. I didn't get the license plate number, but this is a small island. I'm sure we'll find out who did this to us." He stood and held out a hand out to her.

She came to her knees but struggled to stand on her feet. "Aw." She winced.

"What is it? Where do you hurt?"

She dropped to all fours. "I don't think I can stand. My whole body hurts."

"Let me help you." He picked her up like he was going to carry her over the threshold, then he made his way up the hill, back to his bicycle. "I'm going to call someone to pick us up. Please don't move until we can get you checked out." He pulled his phone from his pocket and dialed. The moment Omar answered, Xander barked instructions at him, keeping his eye on Olivia. The confident, straight-talking woman he'd spent the day with had disappeared. She looked like a vulnerable child whose parent was late to pick them up from school.

He sat down beside her. Her hands trembled. "What is it?"

"Someone just tried to kill me!" she yelled.

"I don't think that's what happened." He didn't want to frighten her, but she might be right. How could someone hit both of them when they were several feet apart? He didn't have the answer yet but give it a few days, and someone would be sorry. Very sorry.

"I'll be okay." She straightened her T-shirt back into place. "I just want to go home." Her voice was still several octaves higher than normal.

"Home, New York, or home at the beach?"

"The beach."

"Stay right here without moving?" He took a step away.

She grabbed him. "Are you going to leave me here? Alone?" Her voice shook.

He knelt to get eye level with her. "I'm just going to get your camera and the gift you bought."

"But suppose that…that car comes back." There was panic in her eyes. "Please don't leave me."

"Olivia, look at me." He gave her a calming stare. "That car won't be coming back. I promise you. I'll only be gone a few seconds. Just stay here. Don't move."

She nodded, but the doubt did not disappear from her eyes.

HE BACKED AWAY, holding her attention as he inched toward the ravine and her bike.

He picked up her camera bag and the colorful gift from the shop and made his way back to her side. At least she had taken his advice. The look of disbelief still plastered on her face.

Within minutes, Omar pulled up. Xander picked up Olivia and carried her to the back seat of the car, where she stretched out.

"Where are we heading and who is your friend?" Omar's grin said things he wouldn't dare say aloud. The two of them had a rich history, most of which they couldn't talk about in the presence of others.

"To the clinic. Olivia can't put any weight on her knee." Xander glanced over the seat. Olivia stared at nothing while rubbing her forehead. "Is your head okay?"

She didn't respond, nor did she acknowledge she'd heard him.

"Olivia, is your head okay?" He spoke louder.

She looked up at his face, but her eyes weren't focused.

"What is it?"

She darted her gaze to Omar.

"You can talk in front of him. He's my assistant. I can vouch for him."

"I don't think what happened back there was an accident," she said.

"Sure, it was. Why would someone hit us on purpose? We could have been killed."

She brushed grass off her knees. The car was quiet, waiting for her next reply.

"I left New York to get away from drama." Her voice was low. He had to strain to hear her. The tense draw of her mouth was all the indication he needed to know she was serious.

Omar pulled to a stop in front of the clinic.

"Omar, go back to the site. Pick up the bikes. You'll find hers in the ravine a few yards from where you picked us up. Take some measurements and some pictures. You know the drill."

"Sure thing, boss. Anything else?"

"I'll call you when we're ready to leave here. I'm going to want a full report."

"Should I contact the police?"

"No, not yet. I want to know what we're working with before I involve the authorities."

"Don't you believe me?" Olivia's full vocal range was back.

"I do." He chose his words with care. "I'd like to have more information before I get anyone else involved. That's the way I like to work."

CHAPTER 10

This was not happening. There was no way this was happening.

Not here.

Not to her.

Not again.

Olivia balanced the clipboard on her knees to sign her release documents. Her signature wasn't recognizable. She couldn't steady her hand. When the car rammed her off the road, her stomach had knotted, and her heart had adopted a new rate that wasn't close to normal. It wasn't getting any better. The nurse said it was expected after the tumble she took.

She glanced across the room at Xander seated in the hard plastic chair in the corner. "I'm glad you're here with me. If I were going through this alone…I don't know what I'd do."

"I have a habit of being in the right place at the right time," he said without looking up from his phone. He paged through and tapped on several screens. The scratch on his upper cheek sported a small bandage that gave him even more of an edgy look.

"Were you hurt?" she asked.

"No. I was beyond the guardrail, and on a flatter surface, so this is my only souvenir." He pointed to his cheek.

Something was on his mind. His mood had changed. David had been adamant that she keep her circumstances for being on the island private. But how could she let Xander think what happened earlier was just a coincidence?

"While we're waiting on your instructions, tell me a little bit more about the drama you left behind." Xander leaned forward to place his elbows on his knees.

"There isn't a lot to tell. I don't know who it is. But twice he managed to get in my place. The last time was pretty scary."

Xander pulled his chair closer.

"When I came home, he'd spray-painted my walls. My friend thought it would be best if I got away for a while."

"Do you know who this person is?"

"No. Everyone thinks it a man, so I say he," she said.

"This friend—is he a boyfriend?"

"No, more like a brother. Even though I have two broth-ers, David is the person in the city I call for advice. He's NYPD. He's doing some investigating while I'm here."

"And you think someone has followed you here to Sebastian?"

She pushed her hair off her face. "I don't know what to think. Last night I heard...I thought I heard...maybe I heard something on the porch."

"Something like what?"

"I'm not sure. I woke up to the sound, and I was afraid to get out of bed to check. It could have been a huge iguana. They seem to be like pets around here." She hunched her shoulders. "But what happened today—with the car—I have no questions about that."

He reached for her hand and squeezed. "We'll figure this out."

The doctor entered the room. He instructed her to stay off her knee as much as possible for a few days then, handed her a small vial. "These are for the pain. The nurse has already given you one. They may make you a little groggy, so don't drive when you're taking them. You'll probably be more uncomfortable tomorrow than you are today, so take the pill as needed to stay ahead of the pain. Any questions?"

She shook her head. "I understand."

Xander said, "Don't worry. I'll help you. You're not alone." He rubbed her back.

"If you can get me back to my place, I'm sure I'll be okay." She hopped off the bench, coming down on her uninjured leg.

"I don't think that's a good idea. Let's find out what's going on first. You can stay with me tonight." He helped her into the wheelchair that an aide had brought into the room. "We'll come up with a plan tonight."

Alarm bells rang in her head. She could hear David telling her this wasn't a good idea. And she would agree with him. She didn't know Xander well enough to stay with him, but going back to her place alone was just as scary. "Let's just get out of here."

By the time they pulled into the drive leading to Xander's house, the sky had turned deep blue, almost purple, with just the right amount of gold streaks to add drama. The sun rested on the horizon.

"Ohhhh, look at that beautiful sunset." She pressed her nose against the window of Omar's car, leaving a smudge.

"Are you okay, Olivia?" Xander asked.

"I'm just fine." She sang the words like a child spinning on a merry-go-round.

Xander gave Omar some instructions before carrying her

inside as if he'd been doing it for months, and she held on to him like a woman expecting nothing less. Now wasn't a time to worry if she was too heavy for him. The two of them had been in an accident today. They'd formed an invisible bond around the afternoon's events. In this crisis, Xander took charge and mapped out their next steps.

Her thoughts were jumbled, and her head felt as if it were full of cotton balls. She giggled in his ear.

"Is everything okay?" he asked.

"Yeah. I'm feeling better already." She rubbed his earlobe between her index finger and thumb. "You have nice ears. They're a nice size. Not too big or too small."

"I think your pain pills are making you loopy."

"I think your pain pills are making you loopy," she mocked him, but her voice was artificially high. "I'm not loony. In fact, I'm feeling like a million bucks. Just like your chest. Do you know you have more muscles than Superman?" She kneaded his pecs and talked into his neck.

He deposited her on the sofa, but she continued to keep her arms around him as she tried to pull him down. "Don't you want to sit beside me, handsome?" She kissed his lips. She would have stuck her tongue into his mouth, but he stepped back.

He chuckled. "I think you should get some rest."

"Your house is quite different from the place I'm renting. Instead of the usual, renter quality furnishings, your place is high end." She waved her hands, similar to the way her Aunt Hen did after a bottle of wine at Thanksgiving dinner. Olivia wanted to dial back her behavior and the volume of her voice, but she couldn't control either. "Where is the snap-together furniture and embroidered pillows telling me how lucky I am to be at the beach?" She glanced around the room. "Am I slurring my words?"

"A little bit. I live here all the time. I don't need a

reminder."

"You must like white. Everything in here is white, a clear indication no small children live in this immaculate house. This is a mini-mansion. I'm talking too much, aren't I? I can't stop." She pushed up on her elbow. "You are quite a handsome man. Do you have a girlfriend?"

"No."

"Do you want one?"

"Are you available for the job?"

"I'm only here for a week, but what the hell—"

"Maybe I ought to ask you that question again when the pain meds have worn off."

"You better take advantage of me while you've got the chance. There is no telling what freaky stuff I just might do. I haven't had sex in over a year."

"Even though the offer is tempting. I can't take advantage of you."

"I sure would like to take advantage of you." She kicked off her sneakers and propped her feet on the arm of the sofa. She dropped her head back and closed her eyes.

THE SMELL of citrus stung her nose. She stretched her arms and legs, extending her body. "How long was I asleep?"

"About an hour."

"My head feels heavy."

"I'm sure it's the pain pills."

Bits of conversation crossed her memory. She'd been flirting. "Why do I get the impression I did something I'm not going to be very proud of?"

"You didn't do anything, but you said some pretty risqué stuff."

"Oh no. Like what?"

"Don't worry about it. But, later, I might hold you to some of the promises you made."

"Promises like what?" She fluffed the back of her hair.

"I'll remind you later."

She climbed off the sofa and placed her feet on the floor, testing her knee. Through the window, she could make out the roof of her rental place. His ability to spy on her was effortless with this view. The smell of money was in the air. This wasn't the house of a man with a modest income.

"Where are my purse and camera?" She looked around the formal living space.

Xander pointed to the table beside the sofa. She pulled her phone from her camera bag. "I need to call David. I have to tell him what's going on."

"I'll give you some privacy." Xander strolled out of the room.

David's phone rang twice before he picked up.

"I was run off the road today," she said without greeting him.

"Slow down, Olivia. What happened?"

She told him the story, trying not to leave out any details. "How could he know where I was? We made all the arrangements for this trip using Eva's phones, Eva's computers. The only person who knows I'm here is my family. I didn't even tell Ajay and Gwen."

"Where are you now?"

"I'm at Xander's place. We were riding our bikes together when it happened."

"Who is Xander?"

"Long story. We had a mix-up at the airport when I arrived. He lives on the hill in the house just above the one I'm renting. The car hit him, too, but he's okay. Better than I am."

"What happened to you?"

"I twisted my knee. The doctor told me to take it easy for a few days, but I don't have any broken bones, and I didn't tear any tendons or ligaments."

David was quiet for several seconds.

"Are you there David?"

"Yeah. I don't think what happened here is related to what happened today. That would be almost impossible. There is no way he could have hacked Eva's computer and gotten there so fast. But do you trust this guy you're staying with? Is he married or does he have a girlfriend?"

"I trust him. He seems like a straight-up guy. At least, I haven't seen anything so far in his place that says he's into any sadistic rituals or sex trafficking." She held the phone away from her ear. "Xander, are you married or where are your girlfriends?"

Xander walked into the room, his head tilted to one side. "I'm not married, and right now there is no girlfriend. Why?"

She relayed the information to David.

"Text me his name and his address. I'll take a look to see what I can find out about him."

"I already did. Nothing." Was all she said since Xander was still staring at her.

"I'll dig deeper. Olivia," David's voice softened. "Be careful. We don't know this guy, and we don't know what's going on. You can't trust anyone right now." She agreed and ended the call with David.

"Do you trust him?" Xander asked.

"He asked me the same thing about you." She inspected his face, looking for a tell. What she found were reasons to hold him, dear. "I do. David is my friend. He's always there for me."

"Do you trust me?"

"I guess so. I'm not sure why. I hardly know you. But I do, which scares me, too."

CHAPTER 11

*X*ander strolled out of his office to check on Olivia. She was asleep again on the sofa. Her head was back at an angle that looked uncomfortable, but he didn't want to wake her. He leaned against the door jamb. Her story may not have been as far-fetched as it sounded. It was worth looking into. No one should have to live with the threat of a stalker.

Back in his office, he punched the three letters from the license into his computer. There were twenty-eight cars on the island that began with those letters. Four of those vehicles were registered to the largest rental agency at the airport, the same one he saw on the bumper. He stared at the data. Getting this much information usually required a lot more research. Whoever wanted to intimidate Olivia had gone through a lot of trouble if they'd come all the way to Sebastian.

He dialed Omar. "I've got something I want you to check." He provided the rental car data to Omar.

"I'm almost certain an island native wouldn't have paid the higher airport rates when they could have gotten a much better deal from a neighborhood car rental. So, see what you can find out about that driver. Name, home address, flight information, where on the island they're staying. Anything. And if you have to use our other techniques, then do it."

"This is personal, huh?"

"Yeah, it is. Not just for me, but for Olivia, too. I don't want her to get the wrong impression of our beautiful island." He tried to chuckle, but the look Olivia had on her face after the accident stifled the sound. The fear in her eyes was tangible.

"Who would come to the island and run two people off the road?" Omar asked.

"That's what I want you to tell me. We just might solve two mysteries for her today." He spun around in his chair. "Look, I've got to go, Olivia is waking up. Call me if you find out anything, no matter the time."

"A couple of things before you hang up. This Hecker case. Don't forget we're supposed to meet with them next week. I've been searching the court records. The paperwork goes back fifty years, and they have a rightful claim. They may want us to testify on their behalf."

Xander checked his phone. "I've got it on my calendar. I'll be there. What else?"

"Eliza called again about the warehouses. She's questioning how secure they are."

"I'll call her personally. We've got that place under twenty-four-hour surveillance. She must have gold in there with the artwork."

"What did you decide about Jacobs?"

"He's a no-go. He's into some illegal activity, and I don't want to be anywhere near it."

"That's what I thought. I've gotten a few calls from some of Jacob's henchmen, and I'll let them know. We have a few other things to discuss, but they can wait." Omar liked to keep everything tidy. Xander had no time for the little details, so it was good to have him around.

He ended the call.

From the doorway he watched Olivia twitching in a restless sleep. It was time for another pain pill.

She stretched, winced, then opened her eyes.

"How are you feeling?"

"Like an eighteen-wheeler mowed me down."

"That bad." He opened the medicine vial, then handed her a pill with a glass of water.

"Just you wait. By tomorrow morning you might have a few sore spots too. Then you'll have a better understanding of what I'm going through."

"Let's hope not. One of us has to be of sound mind to figure out what's going on."

"We need to call the police—tell them what happened. I don't want to drag you into this…this mess. You have work to do. I don't expect you to stop what you're doing to help me." She sat all the way up.

"I'm not only helping you. I'm helping myself, too. That car also knocked me off the road."

"But if you stay out of this, you should be okay." She bit her lip.

He shook his head. "I can't let you go through this alone. I have to help you."

"I need to get home. I can't impose on you any longer." She tried to swing her legs off the sofa, but he blocked her.

"You can't go home. Not tonight." He put his hand on her shoulder. "We'll contact the police tomorrow. It's no bother. I have an extra bedroom. I'll go down to your place and get you anything you need."

"My head feels like a ten-piece band is practicing for a concert. The thumping is so loud."

He stood. "While you were asleep, I fixed us something to

eat. Let me get what you need from your place, and then we can eat. It might help you feel better."

"Xander, I can't."

"That's settled for tonight. We'll discuss what we're going to do about tomorrow—tomorrow. Tell me what you need from your place." He grabbed pen and paper and scribbled down her list. "You need all that stuff for one night? I thought you'd only say a toothbrush."

"That's what you get for volunteering to help me."

Xander studied the list as he made his way down the hill. He shortened his strides. The soreness that Olivia mentioned was already showing up, but he wouldn't let her know that. He'd need a long soak in a hot tub tonight. In eight short hours, his quiet existence had made a ninety-degree turn. If something had to change, at least Olivia made it less notice-able. He quickened his steps. The night was still; the only sound was the waves washing up on the shore.

With the key to her place pressed into his palm, he entered the porch on the side of the house and made his way to the front door. He was familiar enough with the property to know the porch circled the entire house.

He heard the footsteps, but the blow to his jaw caught him off guard. This was Sebastian Island, a peaceful paradise. He staggered back for only an instant before his instincts kicked in. Even though he couldn't make out a face on the assailant, Xander planted his feet and landed a solid gut punch. The impact of the blow sent the assailant stumbling backward, but not for long. The masked man rushed Xander again, throwing a flurry of jabs. Some landed, but if Xander hadn't ducked just in time, the fist that looked like a sledge-hammer would have landed on his temple. Xander landed a blow to the guy's solar plexus that slightly lifted the assailant off his feet. Without giving him an opportunity to regain his composure, Xander threw another punch to the same area, sending him over the porch rail and onto the sand.

Before Xander could jump over the rail, whoever had been lurking around Olivia's place was halfway down the beach. Xander sized up his assailant. He was twice the size of Xander and probably a few years younger. Xander rubbed his jaw. It was going to hurt like hell in the morning.

He circled the house. There was no sign that the guy had gotten into the house. But for sure, Olivia was right. Their peaceful town had grown some evil roots.

By the time he made his way back up the hill and into his house, his body registered the wear and tear of every blow.

"What happened to you? Your nose is bleeding." Olivia came off the sofa and limped toward him. "Oh my God. I don't believe this."

He hesitated. Telling her would make her feel worse, but he had no choice. He couldn't keep the information from her. "Someone was lurking around your place. We got into a bit of a scuffle. I'm fine."

She expelled a deep breath. Her eyes wide with worry.

"I'm fine, Olivia. Let's get you back onto the sofa."

"I have to clean up your face." She made her way to the kitchen, favoring her knee, but was back in seconds.

She dabbed the corner of his mouth with a damp paper towel. Her touch was lighter than it needed to be. But he appreciated that she thought she needed to be gentle with him. She was inches away from his lips. Close enough for him to kiss. Under any number of other circumstances, he would have taken advantage of her vulnerability and her pouty mouth.

CHAPTER 12

*O*livia stared into Xander's eyes. They were a colorful mix of green and blue. The contrast with his dark hair and the persistent scruff on his chin was more than just a little charming. He was downright sexy. Being this close to his mouth tonight with the pills leaving her half-baked and erasing any restraints wasn't a good idea. The sight of his blood on the paper towel she held to his mouth kept her from being foolish.

"We make a perfect pair, don't we? Me with my sore knee, you with the scratched face and now a bloody nose," she said. "Do you think whoever attacked you was looking for me?"

"I don't know why he was snooping around your place. After he ran off, I went inside, and nothing looked disturbed. I was able to find your computer, your other camera case, and everything else on your list. I don't think he was even trying to get inside."

"What do you think he was doing?"

"I don't want to upset you. Let me handle this."

"Xander, don't do that. Don't treat me like I'm something fragile. Tell me what you think."

He paused for a moment without breaking eye contact. "I think he may have been waiting for you to come home." He touched her shoulder. "But, don't worry. I won't let him hurt you. I promise."

"Xander you can't promise me that. First, you don't know me. Second, you don't even know what kind of crazy this person is suffering from. If you'd seen what he did to my apartment, you wouldn't be so quick to jump in."

With his thumb and index finger, he stroked her chin. "Your stalker doesn't know who he's dealing with, either. You don't need to worry about me."

She hobbled back across the room. "I'm going to call the police." She glanced over her shoulder at him. "You're not going to try to stop me?"

"Could I if I wanted to?"

"No. Does 911 work here on the island?"

"Yes."

She relayed their location information to the operator. "They're sending someone over."

"While we're waiting, let's eat." He stood. "You sit down. I'll get it."

She flopped down at the table in the kitchen. Without trying, she'd managed to bring terror to the most peaceful place on earth that she knew. And now Xander was caught up in it—was hurt too. She couldn't let that happen again.

He came toward her carrying the food on a tray. The aroma of the curried chicken took her to a safe place— summers with her grandparents, her siblings, and the love her family had shared.

"I hope that tastes as good as it smells."

"Of course, it does. I wouldn't serve anything less than my best for my guest. I have an excellent selection of wine, but, with your pain pills, I opted for water for you tonight. Or we can have soda."

"Is that what I am? A guest?" She glanced down at her hands, unable to hold his steady gaze. She'd dated enough to know that look. "Are you sure I'm not a nuisance?"

"I'm sure. I've enjoyed every minute I've spent with you today."

If she could have brushed off his words as a casual comment, she would have, but the straightforwardness of each word stirred something in her soul. Something she wasn't quite ready to recognize.

She picked up the fork and dug into the curry. If she kept her eyes on her plate, then he couldn't see her blush.

They'd finished eating by the time his doorbell rang.

"The police weren't in a hurry, were they?" she said.

"We're on island time." He opened the door. "Hey, Jimmie. Come on in."

Jimmie did not resemble the formal image of any police officer she'd ever seen. He wore a green and yellow shirt with a palm leaf print. Instead of pants, his knees peeked from under the hem of his green cargo shorts. He had on a pair of sandals that closed with Velcro straps.

"This is Olivia Sika." Xander nodded in her direction. "We've got a story we want to tell you." Xander sat on the sofa next to her.

"Whatever this story is, it looks like you didn't get a happy ending." Jimmie took the seat across the table from them.

Xander did all the talking. This was his environment. Olivia was used to police officers in uniforms with guns and holster strapped to their waist. This laid-back island attitude was all new to her. Jimmie didn't have a notepad, nor did he take notes. He nodded at critical points as Xander talked. Now and then he glanced over at her for confirmation, so she nodded, too.

Xander finished, leaned back and exhaled.

"What do you want to do next?" Jimmie asked.

Olivia held up her hand. "You're the police, aren't we supposed to ask you that question?" Her words tumbled out of her mouth. Were the two of them poking fun at her?

Jimmie and Xander exchanged a look. "She insisted we call the police." Xander shrugged.

"What is going on here?" Olivia's heart thumped against her chest. Was this a trap? Had she been gullible enough to allow the stalker right into her life? Had she trusted the wrong man, again? They weren't taking her seriously, and if her stalker was now in Sebastian, then she was in more trouble than she'd been in New York.

CHAPTER 13

Olivia eyed the door, calculating the distance and how long would it take her to get there. Trying to reach the only exit she'd seen before Xander or Jimmie could stop her was impossible. She probably couldn't even get to her phone before one of them got to her, and it was lying on the table in front of her.

Xander put his hand on her leg.

She pulled away.

"Olivia, you've got this all wrong," he started. "I work with the police sometimes."

"A lot of the time." Jimmie laughed, slapping his knee.

"I don't mean to insult you, Officer Jimmie, but can I see your badge?"

"Of course." His chuckle sounded friendly. "And please call me Jimmie." He reached into his back pants pocket, pulled out a leather bi-fold, then flipped it open for her.

She took it from him. There was no way of knowing if the badge was real or fake. Jimmie could have picked up his credentials online. How would she know?

She handed the badge back and turned her attention to Xander. "Are you a cop?"

Xander looked across the room at Jimmie. "I'm better." The smile that spread across his face said there was a lot deeper meaning to his words.

"I have a feeling if I asked you what that means, you won't tell me the truth. Or you won't tell me the *whole* truth. So, for now, I'm going to save us all some time. What's next? Should we go to my place and check around? Shouldn't you ask for a description of the car and the person who attacked Xander?"

"It really wasn't an attack," Xander added. "The other guy was the one who ran away. And I can assure you, he looked worse than me."

"Did I disparage your ego?" She reached over and stuck her index finger in his rib, hoping the gesture would convince him she was joking.

"My ego would need more than a glancing blow to be knocked from its solid foundation. You needn't worry about that." He got her joke, but there was more bass in his voice.

Jimmie stood. "While the two of you flirt with each other, I'm going to walk down to the Macklemore place to look around. I've got a flashlight in the car. I'll see if he left anything behind. I'll check in with you two lovebirds tomorrow."

Olivia put her hand up. "Jimmie, we're not lovebirds. We're barely friends. I just met Xander yesterday."

"Uh-huh?" Jimmie snickered on his way out the door.

"He's a policeman here on the island? You guys are in trouble." Olivia folded her arms.

"Don't underestimate Jimmie. Just because his attire is laid-back doesn't mean his skills are."

"I didn't mean to insult your friend. I'm sorry. I'm just used to very formal officers."

The smug look on Xander's face wasn't amusing. Her life was in crisis, and he couldn't have been calmer.

"You must know something I don't know. For a man in a brawl tonight, you should be furious." She stopped to scrutinize him. What did she know about Xander Fitzgerald? Almost nothing and yet she planned to sleep under the same roof with him tonight. She couldn't get much more vulnerable than going to sleep with a stranger just a few feet away. But if he wanted to hurt her, he'd had plenty of time. Fear was taking over. She could feel it creeping up her spine. If she didn't get herself together, she'd be afraid of her reflection.

"I think now is a good time for us to get real with each other," she said. "Tell me what you do—for a living. You never answered when I asked earlier."

"I'm run a protection business."

"Protection business, what does that mean? Is that like a bodyguard?"

He picked up his glass and took a sip of water. After setting it back on the table, his eyes narrowed.

"Just tell me the truth. I can see you're trying to think of what to say."

"In simple terms, I guess you could say I'm a bodyguard. But I guard more than bodies, and the protection I offer is a lot more sophisticated than following people around and keeping the paparazzi at bay."

This time it was her turn to sip water. "I see."

"I'm sure you don't."

"Tell me, then, what I need to know."

The corners of his lips turned up. "The less you know, the better. Many of my customers require absolute privacy and anonymity. I work on the right side of the law, but just barely, and that's the way I want to keep it." He leaned forward. "I can keep you safe and I will. I think your stalker may have just come across the wrong person."

The conviction in his tone was the most reassuring thing she'd heard in months.

"Why would you get involved? I don't understand."

"I can't stand to see a woman being intimidated. You shouldn't have to live while looking over your shoulder all the time."

His words were comforting. He sounded convincing enough to help her breathe without added worry. Maybe Xander could do what she and David couldn't.

CHAPTER 14

*X*ander jumped up. "Would you like another glass of water?" he asked on his way out of the room. She asked good questions. But that didn't mean she was going to get his most honest answers. Not since Hope had he poured his heart out to a woman—to anyone—and Olivia's mesmerizing eyes weren't going to change his mind.

The most important thing right now was to keep her safe and connect the dots to find out what was going on. One thing he knew how to do well was solve problems, and right now she needed results more than she needed a lover.

He pressed the glass against the water dispenser on the refrigerator. The sound of her behind him wasn't surprising.

"You didn't answer my question. I need to know why you want to help me. If this had happened last year, then maybe I wouldn't be so persistent about an answer, but now I have to question everything and everybody. I need to know." She stood beside him.

"What I do is in my blood. It's as natural for me to protect people as it is for you to snap pictures."

"I can't pay you."

"I'm not asking for money."

"I won't have sex with you."

"I haven't asked you to. Yet."

They stared at each other for several high-intensity moments. He wanted to kiss her. Just once. Maybe once would satisfy his curiosity.

"So we have an understanding?" She took a step back.

"Yes. I'm going to do what I do best, and you're going to let me." He placed his hand on her arm and steered her back into the living room. "Now, I need you to tell me everything your stalker has done. Don't leave anything out. The more you tell me, the better I can do my job."

"Okay," she said. She reached for her pills, popped one, then sipped from her water glass.

"I know you may not want to relive some of those incidents, but like I said, the more I know, the better."

She laid out the details of the two times the perp had entered her apartment. The roses that she'd snapped in two and shoved into the trash. She mimicked the writing on the walls by making sweeping gestures with her hands. "Let me show you some of the texts I've gotten." She scrolled through her phone before handing it to him.

I want to stop by to see you tonight.

Why are you ignoring me?

We belong together.

I thought about you all nigh, with my hand down on my dick.

The messages went on and on. There were twenty and thirty messages a day. Then they stopped.

"Why did he stop sending the messages? Did you block his number?"

She nodded. "At first I thought it was best to know what was going on in his head. But then the messages started getting more graphic and upsetting, so David and I decided it would be best to stop them."

"Did you guys try to trace any of them?"

"Yeah. A burner phone."

He rubbed his chin. "Any social media contact?"

"He hacked all of my social media accounts. Posted inappropriate pictures and posts. I shut them all down. Do you want to see?"

"Don't worry. I'll get all that information."

She tilted her head. Doubt registered on her face. "How, if I don't give you the account information?"

"I have my ways."

"How?"

"Remember I told you there are some things you don't want to know?" He left the room long enough to get an adapter. "Give me your phone. I'll download all the data."

She handed it to him, but the look on her face showed her skepticism. Within seconds, the transmission was complete.

She seemed to accept his answer—or maybe recalling all the details was too much for her. She collapsed on the back of the sofa, deflating like a three-day-old balloon.

He gave her a minute to absorb everything that was happening. "Are you uncomfortable, now."

"My knee is fine. Those pain pills are strong. It's my life that's making me uncomfortable, now." She cleared her throat. "I can't continue living this way. This thing has morphed over my life. Nothing is easy or simple anymore. I don't sleep through the night because I have to be alert. I'm afraid to take a call unless I know who the caller is. I can't go somewhere unless I've done a thorough survey and know I will be safe and who will be there." She pounded her fist on the table next to her.

"I want to draw this person out, and I think I've come up with a way to make that happen."

She sat up. After he propped her foot on the pillow, he took the seat beside her.

"Tomorrow, you and I are going to go down to the beach. We are going to pretend to be a couple." He waited for her reaction. When there wasn't one, he continued. "We'll take pictures of each other, swim a little, and pretend we're together. Since your stalker thinks you belong to him, seeing us together might lure him out to fight for you. By testing his possessiveness, we could drive him nuts. He might show up right there, demanding I unhand his woman."

"Suppose he does? What will we do, throw sand in his eyes?"

"You underestimate me, sweetheart. If he shows up, he'll wish the only thing he got was a little sand in the face."

She shook her head. "Do you think this will work? It sounds a little flimsy to me."

"We'll give it a try. If that doesn't work, I'll come up with something that does."

"How are you going to protect me—us? I'll feel like a deer standing in an open field during hunting season."

Olivia wasn't the first woman to question his abilities, but she was the first woman to wonder if he could protect her. Hope had said he didn't have enough capacity to love anything other than his work. Hope had said she'd felt safe with him, but not loved. Those words had ripped him in two, but maybe Hope was right. Olivia didn't need his love, but she needed his protection. He had to give her the one thing he was skilled at doing.

He walked into his office and returned with his Glock. "Trust me. You can feel safe with me."

"Is that thing loaded?"

"What good is an empty gun?"

CHAPTER 15

Olivia knew her mouth hung open, but with her life spinning away from the familiar, how could she sit on Xander's sofa and pretend what was happening was normal?

The gun in his hand was nothing at all like the guns her father and brother used. Those had been for game hunting, rifles and shotguns. The weapon in Xander's hand resembled something from the late night news.

She put up both of her hands, trying to slow the momentum of the moment. "Wait a minute. Just wait. We're going to sit on the beach. Make believe we are a couple. Lure in a lunatic. Where in your swim trunks do you imagine you're going to hide this gun?" She shook her head, trying to clear away everything she'd just said.

He zipped across the room to her. "You are going to have to trust me. For a woman who is in charge of her life, I know you might struggle with that concept, but give it a try. This kind of thing, I do for a living."

"I think I need another pain pill. If not for my knee, then for my head. Everything is happening too fast."

"Would you like me to show you where you're going to sleep tonight?"

She didn't answer right away. Would she ever be able to shake the odor of fear that was always with her now? Ten years from now would she look back at this time and remember the beauty of the water rushing to shore, or would this memory remain stamped with the stench of fear like a brand?

He reached for her hands and held them tight. "Olivia, you're safe here, with me."

There was confidence in his voice. But didn't all men think they could save a damsel in distress? If anyone were worth believing, Xander would be the one. He resembled a modern-day bad-ass. She shook her head. The weight of the day had worn her thin. "I'm exhausted and just want my pain pills to kick in so I can get a good night's sleep. I don't have the energy to worry about another thing. I have to put my faith somewhere, and, right now you seem better than anyone else."

"I win by default?" He looked disappointed.

She touched his leg, squeezing her fingers around his quadriceps. In the few hours they'd been together, he was worming his way beyond her skepticism. "I'm not sure if getting involved with this case is a win or a loss."

He showed her to the bedroom on the opposite side of the house. There was one large window overlooking the sloping hill. The window was so far off the ground only Spiderman could climb into it. At least that was one less entry point she'd have to worry about tonight. She removed her shoes and shorts and crawled into the bed, pulling the sheet up to her neck.

"Aren't you going to sleep in here with me?" She patted the bed.

"Are you afraid to be in here by yourself?"

"No. But it's been a long time since someone warmed my bed."

"I wish I had a recorder, so you could hear everything you're saying."

"Why, because you don't get offers like this often?"

"No, because you won't remember any of this in the morning. Your meds have a way of loosening your tongue and turning you into someone you're not, or into someone you'd like to be."

"You should jump in here and find out for yourself."

A few moments later she heard Xander bring her bags into the room, but sleep was already taking her.

In the morning, Xander woke her with a gentle knock on the door. She sat up and fluffed the side of her hair before telling him he could open the door.

He stepped into the room, dressed in swim trunks and a light blue button-down shirt that he hadn't bothered buttoning. At least the day was getting off to a good start. "Am I safe to come into this room?"

"Sure. Why not?"

"You threatened to assault me last night."

She put her hand over her mouth. "Did I hit you?"

"Sexually. You asked me to come to bed with you, and I don't think you were talking about sleeping."

She shielded her face. "You're lying. Tell me you're lying."

"I was flattered. I've never had a woman speak her mind with so much passion."

"It was the pills."

"Tell yourself whatever you have to in order to get through the day, but I know deep down inside, you want me." His eyes lit up even before his smile spread across his face.

"The last thing I remember is you bringing in my things. So yes, for the first time in days, I slept as God intended."

He sat on the edge of the bed, but far enough away to let her know his intentions were honorable. "How's your knee?"

From under the sheet, she bent her knee. "Sore. Very sore. I'm not sure how we'll frolic on the beach when I am hobbling like a klutz."

"You are worrying about things that you shouldn't. Your stalker won't see the hitch in your step, he'll only see you having fun with someone, which should draw him out."

She stared at Xander for several moments without blinking. "What you're suggesting is the craziest thing I've heard in a long time. I hope you're right."

He placed his hand on her covered leg. It was only a touch, but they kept touching each other as if they were building toward something. The warmth of his touch whizzed through her body like a bolt of lightning. Spending too much time with a handsome man in close quarters—how long could she keep her horny ego in check?

She scrambled out of bed, forgetting she was only wearing her panties and tank from yesterday. She crossed her hands over her thighs. "Which way is the bathroom?"

He pointed at the door across the room, but he wasn't looking at her face.

When he left, she eased out of the bathroom, dressed, then called Eva.

"David told me what happened yesterday. Are you okay?" Eva asked.

"I am now. But you wouldn't have recognized me yesterday. Can you believe this is happening?"

"No. Have you told your father or brothers?"

"I wouldn't dare. If someone doesn't catch this madman soon, I'm going to have to tell them everything. I might even need your help to convince them I don't need to move back to Philly."

"Who is the person you're staying with? Can you trust him?" Eva sounded as concerned as her father would have.

"I think a better question would be, is he safe with me? The pain pills almost made me attack the man last night."

"Are you sure it was the pills and not your inner vixen just tired of being restrained?"

"He's good-looking, Eva. If I must spend time with someone, I couldn't have picked a better male specimen."

"Send me a picture. You know…just for record keeping." Eva laughed.

She hung up. The smell of food led her to the kitchen. The spread on the counter was big enough for a party of five.

"Wow! You must be hungry," she said after parking herself on the seat at the kitchen island.

"I wasn't sure what you liked to eat, so I prepared a little of everything." He uncovered a stack of pancakes. Next, he uncovered scrambled eggs and bacon. "I also prepared us a light lunch to carry down to the beach. A picnic basket gives us an air of authenticity. What do you think?"

She couldn't give him the quick agreement he wanted, but she nodded slowly. He sat down next to her. His bare knee brushed hers. This time she didn't jump. With him this close, the need to look over her shoulder wasn't her first thought. Even the idea of playing a couple on the beach was starting to sound like a feasible plan.

"What do you want?" He pulled over two plates.

"I'll take pancakes and eggs."

After heaping her plate with four pancakes and a mountain of eggs, he fixed his plate. They faced a window, overlooking the hill to the beach. "With views this magnificent, it only makes sense to have plenty of windows," she said. "Do you always cook for your overnight guests?"

He hesitated. "I think I should say yes to your question, but you are the only person who has ever stayed overnight. I don't do a lot of entertaining. But I'll promise, every time you stay over, I'll cook breakfast for you." He popped a piece of bacon into his mouth. "How about that?"

"Sounds like a good deal." She put her fork down. "I'll need to stop by my place and get a swimsuit for your plan."

"That little bikini you wore the first day?" He half-grinned.

"Not today. Yesterday, I didn't know someone was watching me. Today, I want to be prepared for anything. Just in case."

By the time Xander spread the blanket on the sand just beyond her rental, his plan didn't seem as crazy. The waves ran to the shore. The tame water of two days ago was gone. No one was in the water. A few yards away, another couple sat in low beach chairs at the edge of the ocean. A mother and her two toddlers played with bright red plastic buckets, making lopsided mounds in the sand. The three of them had the same sun-bleached blond hair.

Olivia shielded her eyes. "The water looks choppy."

"The island is going to get the tail end of Hurricane Edward. It's nothing to worry about."

"I don't think I was going to worry until you said not to."

"The worst that will happen is the electricity may go out for a few hours."

She held up her hand. "Okay, I got it. A hurricane is the least of my worries." She flopped onto the blanket, leaving plenty of space between them. Taking pictures of men was something she did without hesitation. Nearly half of all the models she shot were men. She was comfortable with the male physique, able to look at the angles and the lighting and not the physical. But not with Xander. Looking at his chest and calves and thighs and arms stoked every female hormone in her body. There was no way to look at him and not have a sexual reaction. Pretending they were a couple wouldn't be hard because it wouldn't require much pretending for her.

She could almost hear her father's domineering voice reverberating in her ear telling her again her dream job wasn't sustainable, and it was time for her to grow up. How many more signs did she need before heeding his words?

She blocked the thought. If she let them inch over that line, she'd go crawling home and back to law school. For sure, she didn't want to wear a business suit and work in a square office from sun-up to sun-down.

Xander held out his hand. "You have to sit closer to me. Remember, someone could be watching us right now. I want him to think you're madly in love with me. You're used to taking pictures of models. Now it's your turn to be the model."

She scooted closer to him. With his arm draped over her shoulder, he leaned into her ear. "Now that I've gotten a good look at this swimsuit with all those cut-outs I think it's more provocative than the bikini. And now I know yellow must be your favorite color." She could feel his breath on her neck.

She put her palm on his thigh. "How's this?"

"That's a good start. Now stare into my eyes like we've been making love all night long."

"You're kidding me, right?"

"No, I'm serious." He kissed her forehead. His hand moved along her back. The longer his hand stayed there, the warmer she felt. "I want your stalker to know you don't belong to him. I'm trying to force him out of the shadows. He'll only do that when we make him uncomfortable."

"Okay, okay. I know. Play acting is just going to take me a little time." She leaned into him and placed her mouth over his. She slipped her tongue between his lips. The idea started as a joke, but when he responded, the pretend kiss turned into something that was far from make-believe.

CHAPTER 16

*E*ven though Olivia was following his instructions, his body's reaction was one-hundred percent real. When she released his tongue, he said, "Wow! I think you're getting the hang of the idea."

"I'm putting my trust in you. Something I haven't done for anyone in years. This stalker thing has fouled up my life in ways you can't imagine."

His heart twinged at on her words. "We're here on this beach, at this moment, for a reason. What I do for a living is tailor-fit for what you need right now. I won't let you down." He pulled her into his arm and hugged her tight, something he'd wanted to do from the moment he saw her sitting on the beach their first day. "Since I've cooked up this plan and we're going to be on the beach all day, you might as well tell me about yourself."

She pushed her sunglasses up on her nose. "Okay. The basics are, I was born in Philly, but now I live in New York. I have two brothers and two sisters. They all live in Philly. My family is very close, and they don't like the idea of me being alone in the city." She paused. "My father would have preferred I stay in graduate school, but I'm the family rebel because I decided to strike out and do the photography thing. My family doesn't know about the stalker. I guess I'm hoping he'll stop and find a more useful outlet for his time before I have to tell them anything."

"Is there a man in your life?"

"No. Not right now. I had a string of awful dates, so I'm focusing on my work. Something I can control."

"Why Sebastian? How did you pick this island?"

"I used to come here every summer to visit my grandparents. They lived here for several years until they got too old and my father had to move them to the States to keep an eye on them."

"Besides photography, what do you do for fun?" He kept his eyes on her long legs. The suntan lotion made them glisten in the sun.

"Not much." She snapped her head up. "Now tell me about yourself. I've put my life in your hands, and I need to know something about you, too."

He cleared his throat. "You know what I do for a living. I'm not married or engaged, and I don't want to be. I've lived on the island for close to five years now because I needed to get away from the life I used to have. I don't like taking orders from anyone, and I don't like men who pick on beautiful women."

"Sisters and brothers?"

"I have two brothers. My parents live in D.C., always have. That's all there is to tell." He turned his attention to the water. "How is your knee? Do you think you can help me pull off this scheme today?"

"Yeah, I'm up to it. I've got faith in this scheme of yours."

"Then let's get started. First, let's take some pictures. Since that's something you always do, it will look realistic."

She pulled her camera from the bag. "I'll take a few of you. Then I'll let you take a few of me."

He stretched out on the blanket. She stood over him, straddling his hips. He put his hands behind his head and flashed a toothy grin.

The moment she held her camera, she shifted onto another plane. One where she must have closed out the rest of the world. The serene look on her face was nothing like the troubled woman from yesterday.

After she took about a dozen pictures, he jumped up. "Okay, now let me take some picture of you."

"Do you know how to use a camera?"

"Nothing this fancy, but show me what I need to do." He stood behind her, and she went through the details. Now he had an excuse for standing so close. The firmness of her butt wasn't surprising. Her skin was as soft as he'd imagined.

"Okay, I got it. Now strike some poses for me."

She put her hands above her head. Her gold wrist cuffs caught the sunlight. He took a step back, to capture all of her. Her tiny waist and the curve of her hips were as intoxicating as she was. For several seconds he studied her through the camera, taking as much time as he could to examine every inch of her perfection. Her eyes were intense, so dark it was almost impossible to make out her pupils. Those were eyes he wanted to get lost in. He could spend forever looking into them. Until this minute, he'd been willing to bet his life was just perfect. Now, he knew better.

He couldn't match her skill with the camera, but he got the shots he'd like to look at long after the day was over.

"Okay, that's enough." She reached for the camera.

"Let's do a selfie."

"I've got an even better idea. I'll use the timer. We can prop the camera on top of the basket." Without waiting for him to agree, she staged the scene, then patted the blanket for him to sit down.

"Let's make this look believable." He sat down behind her and wrapped his legs around her. He placed his lips on her cheek. The camera snapped.

"Change positions, quick," she said.

They sat facing each other. She placed her forehead against his. He was able to look right into her eyes, into her soul. For a moment, only he had the privilege of seeing the depth of her character.

After the snap of the camera, he jumped up, needing to put a little space between the two them or Olivia would see his bulging embarrassment.

He reached for her hand. "Come on, let's get in the water. I need to cool off."

"Okay, just take it easy with me. I'm dealing with a bad knee."

He scooped her up and carried her into the ocean. She clung to his back like a papoose as they played with each other. But the special moment was when she faced him and draped her arms around his neck and her legs around his hips. His insides almost exploded.

By the time they came out of the water, he was in more trouble than when they'd gone in. His body ached for her. The beach was almost deserted now, except for the mother and her two little girls.

"I'm famished," Olivia said.

"I brought us something to eat." He pulled the cheese, crackers, and strawberries from the basket. He held a strawberry to her lips.

She pulled her hair back. "You're going to feed me?"

"Of course. Isn't that what lovers do?"

"Do you think he's watching? Have you seen any signs of someone?"

"To be honest, I haven't, but that doesn't mean he's not around."

She took a bite of the strawberry, then wiped under her lip. "Well, if that's the case, then let me feed you, too." She held the fruit up to his mouth but pulled it back just before he could taste it.

"Oh, it's like that, huh?" He climbed on top of her and took the berry from her hand. Her giggles were as infectious as everything else about her. Something was happening here. Something he couldn't ignore.

She reached into the basket and removed another piece of fruit, but this time she didn't tease him.

The mother and toddlers folded their sheet and headed toward them.

"Are you two on your honeymoon?" the woman asked.

Olivia looked at him, her mouth half-opened.

"Not yet," he answered.

"Well, you look like a happy couple." The woman grabbed a hand of each of the girls and headed toward a house down the beach.

Olivia stared at her fingers pressed in the sand. "We must have put on a pretty impressive show," she said.

He hadn't been pretending, so the day was a lot easier for him.

CHAPTER 17

*a*n hour later they were seated on the porch of her rental. The ocean breeze didn't do much to cool her warm flesh. Both she and Xander had their feet propped on the rail. She wiggled her toes. The bright yellow polish matched her swimsuit. Olivia smiled when she thought of how Gwen would react to her effort. Gwen would say she was lazy and that it took no effort to match polish with an outfit.

Xander held a glass of cheap white wine Olivia had purchased her first day in Sebastian, while she sipped overly-sweetened lemonade. She tried to remember the last time she'd been this relaxed with someone. Dating required so much energy—the small talk, faking interest if there was none, the awkward end-of-the-night when she wondered if kissing was required or not. But with Xander, everything came easy. At this moment, she didn't feel the need to fill the quiet with chit-chat.

The staged event on the beach was over, but her heart could not discern from make-believe and real life. Xander's touches accentuated the emptiness in her life—no one to share good news with or to welcome her home after a long day or to snuggle up with at night. If only some part of it could be real, everything they did, while leaving an imprint on her heart was merely play-acting.

Xander pulled his chair closer to hers. "Let me see the pictures we took today."

She reached for her camera and turned it on. She pulled up the first shot. He stared back at her from the camera with so much intensity that she wanted to believe he was trying to send her a message. Then she moved to the pictures of the two of them. Her trained eye didn't see two strangers posing for the camera. The way Xander hung his arm around her shoulder with their heads tilted toward each other they could have been a pair of honeymooners. Her breath hitched. She glanced at him quickly, but he didn't seem to notice.

"Wow! Look at us," he said. "These look like pictures from paradise."

Did he see the same connection she saw? Did he wish what she'd captured on the camera's disk was real, too? But he stared at the snapshots, lingering on the ones of her longer than some of the others.

After the last pictures, he said, "We did a good job. I understand now why that woman thought we were honeymooners."

"What happens next?" A repeat of the day would be her suggestion.

"We wait." He pulled his phone from the basket. "I'm going to call Omar to see what he's found out about the car." He was out of his chair and on the beach before she could ask a question.

What was happening here? Maybe there were too many make-believe kisses or three too many hugs. She'd tried to keep her feelings in a little box, with the lid on tight, but she couldn't fool herself. Every single touch had come from her heart. She ran her fingers through her hair, pulling it all back before releasing the curls. If she wasn't careful, what should have been a vacation could turn into a nightmare. There were several reasons why she shouldn't get involved with Xander. He lived here. She lived in New York. He said he didn't want a relationship and she didn't want a long distance one. Besides, she was here to find a photo site, not love. All good reasons. As soon as she was alone, she'd make a list of at least ten. That should be plenty to keep her head level. She pulled her attention away from Xander and walked inside.

Xander started talking the moment he came through the door. "Omar should be here in a few minutes. He has some information on the car that hit us, but he said not to get too excited."

She nodded. "In the States, we let the police do the investigating."

He winked. "The wind is picking up. I'm going to secure the outdoor chairs."

"Do you think the storm will be bad?"

"If those waves are any indication, this storm isn't going to blow over."

"What do I need to do?" Her voice quivered.

"See if you can find any candles and matches just in case the electricity goes out. It's a pretty common occurrence here in the summer, so I'm sure there are some in the house."

In the kitchen, she opened and closed several cabinets before finding a variety of candles under the sink. She straightened and stared out of the window. The small bushes swayed, but the movement was inconsistent with the wind. Why would only two bushes move and not all the low brush on the hill? She stared and held her head still, refusing to become hysterical over every little sound and shadow. The reason for coming here was supposed to help her relax and to get away from the stalker.

She pressed her hip bone into the counter, not sure what she was going to see since the sky was too dark. It couldn't be Xander. He wouldn't need to be that high on the hill. Her heart stood still along with her breath. The bushes move again, along the steepest part of the incline, out of sight. Watching through the darkness was scarier than the unlocked apartment door, because this time, she was the witness. She backed away from the window, trying to keep her eyes on the subtle movement just beyond the house.

She rushed to the porch. Xander was at the opposite end tying the last chair to the porch rail.

"Come here." She waved for him to follow. Her voice as tense as the muscles in her neck.

"What?"

She didn't reply. Instead, she rushed back to the kitchen and pointed out the window.

"What do you see?"

He tilted his head. "What am I supposed to see?"

She peered over his shoulder. "Give it a minute. Something's in those bushes." She pointed again. "Or someone."

He stared out the window. "Who do you think it is?"

"I saw the bushes moving. I'm certain someone was out there. See?" She pointed.

He grabbed his gun and headed out. Within seconds he was in the thick underbrush, climbing the hill, dressed in his swim trunks, without a shirt. His back caught a ray of moonlight that sifted through the moving clouds. Other than her father, brothers, and now David, she wasn't used to men putting themselves in harm's way for her. Xander hadn't hesitated when she needed someone. His courage was chivalrous. Even with the stalker so close, a renewed sense that this saga wasn't short-lived filled her chest. Her life kept shifting. There was no way for her to drop her guard.

She looked around the kitchen for a weapon and pulled a large knife from the drawer.

At the window, it took her several seconds to pick up Xander's silhouette. He was walking toward the house, his steps slow as he continued kicking everything in his way.

She met him as he rounded the porch. "You didn't see anything, did you?"

"What are you going to do with that little knife?" He pointed to her hand as they entered the kitchen.

"I'm protecting myself." She placed the knife on the table and stepped closer to him, examining the scratches on his legs from the bramble. "Did you see anything?"

He shook his head. "Doesn't mean I don't believe you, but, maybe it a cat or an iguana. Whatever it was, we'll handle it." He patted the gun tucked into his swim trunks then locked the door before gathering her in his arms. The gesture was so natural she didn't hesitate to exhale against his chest. "It's okay." He stroked her back and kissed her forehead. "Drawing him out is exactly what we wanted, so we'll keep doing what we've been doing."

"Are we still pretending?" she whispered into his chest.

CHAPTER 18

*X*ander had a way of looking through her. Maybe her eyes did for him what his touch did for her.

"Would you be surprised if I told you I was never pretending?" he said.

Her heart leaped against her chest. "Somewhere in there, I stopped pretending, too." There was a connection between them as if they had been waiting for the universe to bring them together.

"How do I know that's not your pain pills talking? They have a way of banishing your boundaries."

"I haven't taken a pill at all today. My mind is clear, and I have control over all my thoughts."

"Is that right?" He crushed her against his chest, capturing her mouth with his. All the pretend kisses had been well worth remembering, but there was something about this one that set the mark. Maybe, it was because they were on the same accord now, using the same set of standards.

The doorbell rang. She didn't want to let Xander go, but he released her to open the door for Omar, his assistant.

Omar shot a quick glance in her direction. She reached for her beach cover on the back of the chair.

Xander pointed to the sofa. "Let's sit down."

Olivia sat on the edge of the sofa, next to Xander.

Omar started reading from a piece of paper he pulled from his pocket. "The car was rented yesterday morning at the airport. The airport has the highest prices on the island, which makes me think the renter wasn't a local. He returned the car with front-end bumper damage which he paid for in cash. The rental agent said the guy was a middle-aged white guy with a stocky build and a beer gut. I've run down a little information on the guy, just a name. Do you know a Steve Bonner?"

Oliva shook her head. "No."

"I'll keep checking. It could be a phony license," Omar shoved the piece of paper back in his pocket.

Xander turned to her. "You're sure that doesn't sound like anyone you know?"

"No. And the guy who showed up on my condo security camera was thin." She intertwined her fingers. "This is crazy. I don't know what I expected."

"Did you check the flights out of New York yesterday, Omar? How many single men flew in?"

Omar pulled a pad from his back pocket. "Three single men deplaned in Sebastian yesterday. None of them were short, stocky or middle aged. There were several couples with men fitting that description, but I've checked them out and eliminated them as suspects."

"Get some guys and stake out the most popular resorts. See who has rented houses on the island in the last few days and see if anyone fits that description. He should be easy to find."

Olivia put up her hand. "How can you get all this information? What about privacy laws?"

Xander placed his hand on her thigh. The squeeze he gave her was as tender as all the other times. "We have our ways."

Omar shifted his weight toward the door. "The storm may be worse than first predicted. I hope you guys have plenty of supplies."

"I have plenty of stuff at my place. I know the drill—batteries, fully charged phones, and plenty of water," Xander said. "You know I'm always prepared."

"Nobody knows it better." Omar shoved his pad back into his pocket before leaving.

The moment they were alone, Xander turned to her. "Now, where were we?"

She clasped his cheeks. "Right here." This time she initiated the kiss and shut out the surroundings—the winds blowing against the windows, the waves in the distance battering the shore, the threat of some madman who wanted to own her. None of that mattered.

Xander released her mouth. "I thought you'd forgotten—"

"No way." She climbed into his lap, her knees settling into the cushions around him.

"I didn't picture you as an aggressor. I thought you were a little shy." He eased his hand under the strap of her swimsuit and pulled it down her shoulder.

"I don't think I know the definition of shy. What you saw was a woman trying to find a little piece of mind."

"All that talk about wanting to be left alone." He moved to her other strap. "What changed your mind?" With both straps off her shoulders, he exposed her breasts and then cupped them.

"You did." Her words rushed out.

"I'll have to make a note of that. I didn't know I had that kind of power." He slipped his mouth over her nipple.

The warmth of his tongue sent heat up her spine and across her chest. She had the feeling of coming out of warm water. Every nerve in her body tingled making the reality of this moment more significant. She was good at compartmentalizing events in her life, but tonight it was the most important thing for her to do. There was work. There was her family. There was her personal life. Each one was separate and existed without interfering with other. So where did Xander fit in? He wasn't going to be a part of her personal life. Not after this trip. But, she was going to have sex with Xander, but they weren't a couple, and they weren't in love. Someone still wanted to do her harm, and a hurricane was barreling toward the island. For now, she put each one of those things into a neat little place and enjoyed this moment and the pleasure that Xander was unleashing in her.

She leaned forward to kiss his neck. Unlike earlier today when she'd held back a little, there was no reason to resist the urge now. They had admitted to having desires, which opened the door for her to act out on every wishful thought. She tugged at his swim trunks.

He eased his hip off the sofa and drew his trunks down his legs without releasing her. She wrapped her hands around his hardened erection.

He grabbed her hand and held it still. "We have one major problem."

"How can that be? You're a man who is always prepared. You just said so to Omar." She pressed kisses across his cheek on her way to his mouth.

"I don't have any condoms in my basket. Unless you have some, then we're going to have to be creative."

She sat back, then unstraddled him. "My plan while here was celibacy."

Xander pushed her down on the sofa and removed her cover and her swimsuit. He dropped it onto the floor. "Then I'll make a deal with you." He laid her back on the sofa and pressed kisses down her neck and between her breasts. "Let me do what I've wanted to do since I first saw you..." He reached her abdomen and stopped long enough to lick her stomach "...and I promise you that tomorrow, we'll go to my place..." He plunged his tongue into her belly button. "...and I'll let you have your way with me..." He continued between her legs. "In fact, I'll insist on it." When he reached her thigh, he spread her legs and inserted his tongue into her core. His movements were slow and tender, slipping in and out of her as if he wanted to linger there. Each time he entered her body she called out his name. She reached for his ears, the need to touch some part of him was all she needed. Pleasure gathered in the back of her throat, and she emitted small muffled sounds. He promised her more to come tomorrow, but for now, the expertise of his tongue was enough. He pressed into that spot that pulled her hips off the sofa.

Her body tingled with satisfaction. His firm grip on her butt kept her from sailing away. With her eyes closed, her body melted into him. His skilled tongue found that spot between her legs that had been neglected for too long. His movements were slow, a man who wasn't in a hurry to move to the next thing. She tried to calm her breathing to stretch this moment out to forever, but he was waking up her body, a body that had been asleep too long. She couldn't stop the wave of ecstasy taking over. She arched her back and let him take all of her.

CHAPTER 19

*A*long time ago, Xander gave up the notion that life was going to give him everything he wanted. After Hope had decided he wasn't the man she wanted to live with for the rest of her life he'd turned off his emotional life and focused on his business. It wasn't as good as having a woman in his life, but at least his mind and time were occupied.

But just like that, Olivia showed up and had him rethinking everything. They were still on the sofa. He settled his weight beside her, but she refused to let him go. And that was fine with him.

"Are you hungry?" she whispered in his ear.

"Starving," he whispered back.

She loosened her arms, rolled him into the crease, then jumped to her feet. "Let me feed you. I have lots of food in the fridge." She made her way toward the kitchen. "I even had some Ms. Myrtle's Chicken delivered when I arrived."

She didn't bother covering up, which gave him a perfect view of her ass. "How do you know about Ms. Myrtle?"

"Just because I haven't been here in several years, doesn't mean I don't know a thing or two."

He joined her in the kitchen. She'd already removed two plates from the cabinet and was piling them high with beans and rice.

"This night just keeps getting better." He took a seat at the counter. "You're leg must be better. You're not limping as much today." He pointed to her leg.

She grabbed her beach wrap and tied it over her breasts before flexing her knee. After putting the chicken onto the plate, she stuck it in the microwave. She came to stand between his legs. "You've taken good care of me. Now it's time for me to take care of you. First, I'm going to feed you. Then we're going to take a hot shower together; then I'm going to take you into the bedroom and…"

"And what? You're not going to leave me hanging, are you?" He pulled her close and pinched her firm behind.

"That's exactly what I'm going to do. I want you to wonder what I've got planned."

The microwave beeped. Olivia switched out the plate and placed the sizzling food in front of him.

"Eat up. You just might need your stamina."

"You know," he shoved the fork into the jerked chicken. "this might be the most fun I've had in a single night without a condom."

She kissed his cheek. "Do you think that means something?"

"I'm certain it means something. So, hurry up and eat so we can get on with more important stuff."

With the meal completed, he placed the dishes in the dishwasher. She hung by the sink, staring out the window. The wind was picking up, but the rain hadn't started yet.

"Olivia, you don't have to worry about him. I'm here with you." He came up behind her and slipped his hands around her waist.

"I know, but once something becomes a habit, you're kinda stuck with the results."

"I don't think I've ever eaten jerked chicken from Myrtle's in the nude with such a stunning woman before. That's a habit I'd like to like."

"Oh. Eating in the nude is something I used to do all the time before someone started invading my privacy." She reached behind and stroked his penis with both hands.

"How about we take that shower now?" He held her fingers. "If I remember correctly, the bathroom is this way." He led the way to the master bedroom.

Her warm hands ran over his butt cheeks. "Has anyone ever told you your butt should be in pictures?"

"Yeah, just the other day when I was shopping for mangos," he chuckled. "That's not something I hear every day. And I'm fine with that."

In the bathroom, she turned on the shower, more hot than cold, which started to steam up the small room. "Wait right there. I've got a scented soap in my suitcase." She disappeared, but was back in a few seconds, minus the gold cuffs on her wrist, but with a big bar of brown soap.

"I don't want to smell sweet," he said.

"Don't worry, you won't." She pulled him into the glass enclosure that was only big enough for one person.

He palmed her hand, taking the soap from her, and rolled it across one shoulder, then the other. When he reached her breast, he slowed his movement. The nutty scent didn't offend his senses. She stood still like a statue, letting her eyes do all the moving. She scanned him from head to toe, then started the gaze over again.

"I can't remember the last time I've had such a blissful and sensuous day all wrapped up into one. I can't believe all this comes with no strings. Everybody wants something. I was raised to be suspicious." She stepped closer to him, allowing the soap from her body to coat him, then she ran her hands over his pecs, kneading his flesh with her slender fingers.

The seriousness of her tone made him uncup her breasts. There was something in her voice that required his full attention. "I'd say it was the magic of Sebastian, but I think what happened today was a lot more than that. We have a connection. I felt it almost immediately, but you took a little time to come around."

"I've been in too many bad relationships. I also have two older brothers. Growing up, I heard the way they talked about the girls they liked and the ones they didn't care so much about. I learned to be careful." She stepped under the water spray. "Which doesn't explain how I acquired a stalker. I must have messed up somewhere."

"Your stalker may be someone you've never even met. That's pretty common you know?"

She glided her hands across his back, then torso, rinsing the soap away. Afterward, she pressed up on her toes and kissed him. The gesture was enough to bring his whole body to full attention. She went down on her knees. The heat of her mouth on his penis had to be equivalent to sticking his finger in an electrical socket. He hoped she didn't hear his gasp. The last thing he wanted was for her to think he couldn't handle what she was dishing out.

With his eyes closed, the water ran cool against his burning skin. He wanted to ignore the emotions that had stormed through his head. Olivia wasn't just any woman. She could be *the* woman, but she wasn't in Sebastian to stay. The moment her visit was over, she was going to return to New York. This special moment was as fleeting as the storm bearing down on the island. And just like he'd prepared for the high winds and rains, he'd take the necessary steps when his time with Olivia came to an end.

CHAPTER 20

*X*ander climbed into her bed and allowed exhaustion to claim him. He looked down at Olivia and recalled the day they'd had. A well-planned date couldn't have gone better. Olivia appeared to be halfway to sleep. Her hair blanketed the pillow in a mass of black curls. He wasn't good at relationships. At least he was willing to admit that failure to himself. If ever he wanted to break free from that flaw, this would be that moment. Olivia wasn't just any woman. She was already touching his soul like no one ever had.

He reached to the bottom of the bed and pulled the sheet up around her.

"This isn't part of your job description, is it?" Her voice was heavy with sleep, but she managed to keep her eyes open.

"I'm not on the clock." He feathered his finger across her shoulder.

"Sure you are. You've been protecting me since the bicycle thing."

"I'm not on the clock." He repeated. "From the moment we left my house this morning, I've been on a date."

Her eyes opened wider. She sat up. "I don't sleep with guys on my first date, so we'll have to call today something else—our second date since we went biking yesterday, or we can call it an adventure."

"Well, we haven't technically had sex—at least by Clinton's definition—so your standards are still intact."

She rested her head on his chest. Her hair was still damp. "If I ask you questions, will you answer me?"

He exhaled. "I like asking questions better than answering them."

"Play along, okay?"

He flexed one knee. "What do you want to know?"

"Are you a hired assassin?"

"No. You watch too much television."

"In your house, is there a special room with guns on the wall, behind a secret door?"

He shifted, but not enough to disrupt her from her position. "I have a room, but with nothing as dramatic as guns on the wall."

"How many guns do you have?" With her index finger, she made small circles on his chest.

"I don't know. I haven't counted in a long time."

"More than five and less than twenty?" she asked.

"More than five."

"Are you on the island because you're in hiding?"

"You have a lot of questions."

"You didn't answer that one."

"In a way, I'm hiding. But not from the law."

"From who, then?"

"I had a bad break-up with someone I thought I could love. Hope wanted kids, the picket fence, and turkey at Thanksgiving. When I wasn't quick enough to drop down on my knee with the big ring, she dropped me. Now she's married to some big-time D.C. mogul. They have a child, and every other week, her picture is on some society page. I needed to get away from seeing all that happiness." He ran his hand down his face. "Are you happy? Now you know."

"Did you love her?"

"No. Not like she wanted. I was fond of her. I would have done anything for her, but I wasn't ready to commit to forever. Something kept holding me back. I figured there was a reason."

She sat up straight. "Oh, you're one of those guys, huh?"

"I don't know what that means. But I do remember you saying you weren't in a relationship either, which means the two of us are more alike than you might think."

"I'm not with someone because I keep coming across men like you. Men who want all the benefits without the liability. All liaisons are blow-your-mind fantastic in the beginning. There's always lots of talking, laughing, fun. But four or five months in and everything changes. Maybe it's the effort of making decisions, what's for dinner, where to spend the holidays, what color to paint the wall, that rips the life out of love."

"Or maybe we just haven't found the right person yet. When two people are meant to be together, even shopping for paint and choosing between Italian or Mexican for dinner can be fun."

"Yeah, but we have no way of knowing, do we?" She settled back under the sheet. "One more question."

"I'm ready."

"Have you ever killed anyone?"

He didn't answer as quickly this time. She'd moved to an area he didn't want to go.

"On the advice of counsel, I'm taking the fifth," he said.

"Here I was hoping you'd say yes."

"We don't need all the answers tonight. I'll give your relationship premise more thought in the morning," he whispered.

He massaged her back until her breathing became even. He climbed out of bed, happy to have escaped her interrogation. At least for now.

In the kitchen, he put the leftover chicken back into the refrigerator, then pulled his swim trunks back on and picked up his Glock from the kitchen table. With the gun at his side, he turned off the light and stood in the darkened kitchen staring at the pitch-black hillside. Who'd been out there earlier?

The probability of her stalker coming to Sebastian didn't add up for him. Some punks would have stayed in the city, preying on someone else until she returned. Why would her stalker attack him? Why take that chance?

He opened the sliding glass door and stepped outside. From the crushed grasses he'd seen on the hill, someone was there, but telling her would have only alarmed her. His job was to keep her safe and find the punk that wanted to scare her. And he would.

The wind was getting stronger, but the rain hadn't started yet. He stood still, allowing his ears to adjust to the roar of the surf. He knew how to ignore that sound and listen for the important ones. But, the wind made it impossible to hear anything else. His gut told him to keep her close and sleep with his eyes open. He'd protect her. Of this, he was confident.

He walked back inside and locked the door. A quick survey of the premises—everything appeared to be in order. In the bedroom, Olivia hadn't moved. He crawled back into bed beside her. If he wasn't going to sleep, there was no better place to do it than beside her naked body.

In the morning, the wind was stronger, and the sound of rain pelted the bedroom window. The sound hadn't stirred

Olivia. She was as glorious in her sleep as she was wide awake. He didn't want to disturb her. After the evening they had, they both could use a little more rest, but sleep passed him by. The weather was only going to get worse. They needed to lock her place down and head up the hill. The Macklemore house was prone to flooding.

He kissed her cheek. Her eyes fluttered open.

"You're up early," she mumbled.

"I didn't want to wake you, but we need to get to my place."

She scrambled to sit up. "What's wrong? What happened?"

"Nothing, but the tide is getting rough, and the wind is picking up. We'll have everything we need at my house. Besides, if the tide comes in a few more feet, this place is going to take on some water."

"I kinda wish we could stay here. The two of us, here, alone, has been like a fairytale."

"I promise, we'll continue our fairytale, in a safer place." He ran his hand over her butt. "You pack up some clothes. I'll make sure everything is secure here."

At least Olivia wasn't one of those women who took hours to dress. Twenty minutes later, she walked out of the bedroom with a large hobo bag stuffed full. She wore a long African print skirt with a slit that ended well up her thigh. The yellow and white tank was a perfect match to the skirt and her bold necklace. She looked picture perfect, but there wasn't time to linger on her appearance. He didn't want to alarm her because she was jumpy enough, but getting back to his place was mandatory.

"Ready?" he asked.

"Yeah. Do you think you need to check around before we go out there?"

He couldn't suppress his grin. "Oh, after a night of sex now you want to tell me how to do my job?"

She put her hand up. "My bad. Yesterday, I was in a horny haze. Today I'm back to reality."

"Go back to the horny haze. I'll take care of reality." He opened the door and stepped out first before waving her to come out. "How was that? Does this match your vision of what personal protection would do?"

"Yeah, you're really good. I like a wise-ass." She kissed him on the way out the door.

The wind and rain had picked up along with the wind. He helped her up the hill, the two of them barreling forward with their heads down.

"I thought hurricanes were unusual for Sebastian."

"They are. But now and then we get some strong effects from a storm. Never a direct hit. I think this one is going to cause a temporary hiccup. It might send your stalker under-cover for a while."

"That's good, right?" She glanced at him with hope in her eyes.

"No. We want to draw the asshole out and keep him there." He juggled the basket in his hand to put his arm around her waist. He kissed her, taking his time even though the rain stung his bare legs.

"You're going to do this now? Kiss? What the hell is happening?"

"Two things. I kissed you because I wanted to and if we're being watched, then that's just an added benefit."

Water drops were visible in her hair. "You're just taking advantage of my situation. But I like it."

"If you think I'm taking advantage now, just wait and see what I have planned for you later." Xander glanced over his shoulder, certain he'd seen someone at the bottom of the hill a moment ago.

CHAPTER 21

*K*eeping pace with Xander back to his place was difficult. The wind blew in their faces, getting stronger with each step they took. Xander only wore his swim trunks. His bare chest was like a wall against the elements. The growth on his face had thickened overnight, and the lines around his mustache and sideburns weren't as defined as they were the yesterday, but didn't distract from his good looks.

Even though Xander carried her bags, she had insisted on handling the camera equipment. Now she wished she'd let him handle everything. He had the muscles to make it easy.

Before Xander turned on the lights in his place, her phone rang. She held up her finger for him. "This is my assistant. I have one of those, too. I need to take this." She slipped into the room ahead of him. "Hey, Gwen, what's up?"

"How's your vacation going?"

"Great. I saw where *Beauty Bar* deposited the funds in the account," Olivia said.

"They liked the pictures. I knew they would."

"I was hoping for another contract. I sent the fashion

director pictures from the island the day I arrived. I'm hoping they'll think about doing a location shot here for one of their issues next year."

"Are you okay? You sound funny."

Yeah, something was wrong, but telling Gwen would make *her* worry. Besides, Gwen had to be tired of hearing about her troubles by now. And how could she say, she was attracted to a guy she'd just met. Xander was practically a stranger. She hardly knew the man. What she was feeling was an overwhelming swell of gratitude for everything he was doing for her.

"I'm fine, Gwen. I'm in paradise. Stop worrying about me and enjoy your free time. How's Ajay?" Telling Gwen only half the truth was wrong, but she didn't want to think about work right now. Enough going on already. Managing all the strands of her life was like trying to hold onto balloons in a high wind. She sighed. She'd explain everything to Gwen when she got home.

"I haven't heard from Ajay since you left. He's probably out with one of his women. Or maybe he's trying to top his last venture of two in one night." Gwen laughed through her last sentence.

"I'd better go. I'll call you tomorrow." Olivia clicked off just as Xander stuck his head in the room. He'd changed out of his swim trunks into a pair of shorts and a white tee. Only he could put on something so simple and make it look good.

"Is everything okay?"

"Yes." She jumped up. "How can I help you?"

He repositioned the large box in his arms. "There is another box on the kitchen table. Can you grab it and follow me?"

She found the box. "What is all this stuff?"

"Water, candles, hurricane lamps, and some snacks. I'm

moving this stuff into the media room. It's an interior room, so it's the safest place for us to be in the storm."

His media room had six leather recliners each with two cup holders. A projection screen in the front of the room took up the entire wall, and built-in speakers were positioned throughout the space. On the left was a well-stocked bar that sported premium brands of every liquor, a wine fridge, and a bright red popcorn popper. In the corner was an oversized bag she hadn't seen him bring in. The odd shape made her curious, but now wasn't the time to ask questions.

"Wow. You are prepared."

"I have a generator, which might come in handy and my place is ideal because it's too high on the hill to have to worry about flooding."

With the boxes unpacked, Xander shoved his hands into his pants pockets. "I'm going to try to cook us something filling that we can eat cold if we have to."

"What do you know about cooking?"

"Oh, don't tell me you're going to tag me with some sexist comment." He placed both of his hands over his heart. "Who do you think cooks for me?"

"Don't you have one of the nice women on the island come in to cook for you?"

He grabbed her by the waist, pulled her into a bear hug then kissed her. His playfulness was as surprising as everything else happening between them. "Come on, let me show you how I make a mean Italian tortellini salad. It's going to be so good you'll beg for my recipe."

"I wouldn't count on that. Cooking's is not my thing, but I'll clean up the kitchen afterward. How about that?"

"You've got a deal." He parked her at the kitchen table. Watching him prepare the meal was a wonder. His moves were as stealthy as everything else he did. Watching him chop the meats and the vegetables was like watching a television chef.

The lights dimmed for a moment, then brightened again. He pointed to the ceiling. "Stick with me, kid. I've been to this rodeo before, which is why I'm cooking now."

Olivia filled the sink with sudsy water and washed the utensils as he finished with them. From the window, the weather seemed to worsen. The darkening sky didn't faze Xander. The windows rattled, then the house grew quiet as if the hurricane had changed course. But, then the winds came back stronger than before.

Xander finished preparing the meal, then transferred it to a large bowl with a lid that snapped close. "Let's get into the media room. If the power goes out the generator will give us lights and power in there." He balanced the bowl in one hand as they made their way through the house. "There is nothing else we can do until the storm is over."

"You're mighty calm about this."

"It's summer in Sebastian. This storm is a small inconvenience for all the sunshine and nice weather we get almost all year round."

After they finished the meal, Xander gathered the dishes, stacking them into a haphazard pile.

"You're going to drop something. They're tilting."

"No, I do this all the time."

The moment he stood, the plates shifted. The noise they made when they hit the floor was deafening.

She couldn't help but smirk before jumping up. "Let me help you clean this up."

He stooped and began picking up the shards of glass. "That's what I get for showing off, right?"

"I'm not going to say I told you so. I'm not that girl."

He stopped gathering the broken pieces and stared at her. "You're my kind of girl." He grinned. "I'll tell you what. While

I clean up this mess, why don't you rest for a moment?" He pressed his lips to her forehead before carrying the dishes away.

He returned, rubbing his hands together and said, "Would you rather listen to some music or watch a movie?"

"A movie." She settled into a chair on the front row and tucked her feet under her.

"Okay, but please tell me we don't have to watch some sickening romantic comedy." He sat in the recliner next to her.

"If that's your preference, then I'll suffer through with you, but I'd rather watch something action-packed," she said.

"My kind of girl." He picked up the remote and aimed it at the huge screen. It came to life, and he scrolled through the guide. "I'm going to pick a classic. *Scarface*."

"All right. And if I weren't full already, I'd want popcorn to go with this movie."

"I can get some. We can have it in less than five minutes." He was almost out of the seat.

The opening credit rolled.

She stopped him. "No. I'm full. I can't right now."

The loud crash in the distance made Olivia crouch in the seat. "What the—" she whispered.

Xander was out of his seat. He reached for the bag stashed in the corner and unsnapped the locks. He flipped the lid on the bag, exposing several weapons. "Stay here." He pulled a handgun from the satchel, removed the safety and checked the chamber. Next, he extracted an oversized switchblade and shoved it into one of the pockets on his shorts.

Her heart pounded against her chest. "Why do you have so many guns? That's an arsenal."

"To protect you."

"Where's the Glock?"

He handed the gun to her. "Do you know how to use a gun?"

"Yes, but—"

"We don't have time to discuss this, Olivia. When I walk out, lock the door behind me and don't let anyone in. Not even me. I have a key. Be ready to shoot anyone other than me who comes through that door."

She stared at him. His words should have made sense, but she struggled with the concept. She couldn't shoot anyone. "You're kidding, right? Look at my hand." She extended her arm, but she couldn't hold it steady. "Stay here with me."

He gripped her shoulder, digging his fingers in just enough to get her attention. She forced her head up to see his eyes.

"Olivia, calm down." He spoke each word slowly as if she was an uncomprehending child. "You'll be okay if you do what I say."

With the gun clutched in his palm, he made his way to the door. "Lock it."

CHAPTER 22

With a quick backward glance at Olivia, Xander stepped out of the theater room and listened for her to lock the door.

He lived for opportunities like this.

He trained for opportunities like this.

His blood pulsed for opportunities like this.

The fear in Olivia's eyes made this time more difficult. He seldom worked for loved ones or people he had an emotional attachment to. Instead, he handed them over to other colleagues in the business. But Olivia had landed in his life, and his heart and her problem were now his.

He crept along the wall leading toward the rear of the house. The sound came from there. He inhaled through his nose and exhaled from his mouth. Olivia's terrorizer had a lot of game if he was willing to come onto an unknown property. Xander stepped around the corner, his weapons secure in his hand. Shadows from the palm trees played against the walls drew his attention; distracted him.

He lowered his arms and relaxed his shoulders. The storm made so much noise there was no way to hear anything else. With the gun back at chest level, he continued to the rear of the house. At the bedroom door, he paused. A gust of wind brushed across the tops of his bare feet. Blood coursed through his veins like foot soldiers. He rushed into the room, his hand on the trigger.

There wasn't much furniture in the room—a bed and a dresser. The window was broken. He dropped to his knees and searched under the bed. On the opposite side of the bed, glass sparkled on the floor, along with the remains of a sugar apple from the tree outside. Xander stood. With caution, he crossed the room. At the window, he stared out into the darkness. The sugar apple tree had snapped at the root and was leaning against the house. He released the air in his lungs. If he'd allowed the gardener to take down the tree weeks ago when his crew had discovered the decay this could have been prevented.

He collected two towels from the linen closet and shoved them into the broken window. The elevation on this side of the house made it impossible for anyone to get in. They'd need a twelve-foot ladder and in this storm, a psychiatric evaluation.

Before returning to Olivia, he surveyed the rest of the house. Everything was intact.

"Olivia, I'm coming in!" he yelled before unlocking the door.

She was on the floor beside the case of weapons, her back against the wall. "Are you okay?" she asked.

"I'm fine. It was only a tree near the house."

"Are you sure?"

He eased the gun out of her hand and placed it back in the case. "Yes. I searched the entire house." He cupped her face. "What were you going to do?" He nodded to the guns.

"Use every one of them if someone tried to come in here."

"That's my girl." He pressed his mouth to hers. She parted

her lips. The eagerness in her acceptance was the only urging he needed. With a deftness he'd mastered in college, he had them undressed and her flat on the floor in seconds.

She slipped her hand inside his pants. Her warm touch relaxed every muscle in his body.

"While I was roaming around the house, I lifted these from my nightstand." He held up a sleeve of six condoms.

"You keep that many in your nightstand drawer? What are you, the island gigolo?"

"Oh, don't tell me you aren't happy I thought of everything. You haven't released my penis since I took off my pants."

"Is that a complaint?" She planted kisses on his neck and shoulders.

With his teeth, he ripped open the foil package. She took it from him and rolled it into place, teasing him every inch of the way. When she finished tempting him almost beyond his ability to withstand the sensations, she pulled him down on top of her. "Enough talking." She wrapped her legs around him and guided him into her.

The tension from earlier disappeared. The only thought he could retain was pleasing Olivia. Their lovemaking yesterday was exceptional, but, this time was the decadent dessert at the end of a gourmet meal. His slow movements were precise, and her moans told him everything he needed to know about pleasing her. He used her unspoken directions to drive her out of her mind with pleasure, until she tightened her legs, pulling him deeper into her sweet folds, consuming his body like fire.

Her sexual appetite matched his and he reveled in the perfection they'd found...together.

CHAPTER 23

*O*livia blinked several times, grasping for the edges of reality. Xander lay beside her. His breathing sounded content. Things were happening so fast. Running into him at the airport, their trip to the lavender farm, being hit by the car, Xander coming to her rescue, and the biggest surprise of all, her feelings for him. Everything rushed back, in a blur of activity that made her heart thump harder.

Outside, the wind howled, making the Santa Ana's winds seem like a summer breeze. At least his media room was cozy and safe. No windows, no need to look over her shoulders, nothing to fear except her escalating emotions for Xander. The quick getaway to Sebastian was turning into something significant. There was no way she was going to leave this island and her feelings for Xander behind.

Xander's breathing was just as rushed as hers. A gradual smile brightened his face.

"Hey, good-looking," He pulled her closer, so naturally that those awkward moments new couples often had to navigate weren't an issue for them. From that conversation on the beach yesterday, the two of them had locked steps like instant lovers.

Xander was the easiest 'almost relationship' she'd ever had, but she had to be careful of thinking of them as a couple. Neither of them had uttered any words that sounded like commitment, relationship or dating, and as long as she remembered they weren't any of those things, she'd be un-heartbroken.

She smiled at him, not sure what to say. "Hey yourself. I thought you were falling asleep. I must be too much for you."

"Either that or I'm exhausted from the marathon make-out session we had last night. A man does need to get some sleep." He adjusted his position, pushing up on his elbow. "How's your knee?"

"Good as new." She flexed it.

"You've got a nice pair of legs. Do you know that?"

"They get me where I want to go, but if you think they're nice—"

His slow nod and the unfocused gleam in his eyes said he wasn't listening. He pressed his hand against her raised leg, rubbing it up and down.

"What are we doing, Xander?" She couldn't hold the question back even though she wanted to. Questions like that were the one sure way to send a man running and no matter how carefree she started out being she always ended up in the same place—want more.

"Waiting out the storm. It's a normal activity in these parts in the summer."

"No. I'm talking about you and me. We're cuddled up on your media room floor like we're a couple with a future. We could be heading toward dangerous territory."

His body stiffened. He didn't move away from her, but there was a shift in the room that had nothing to do with the storm.

"Are you looking for a label to put on us?" His voice was an octave deeper.

She swallowed. She was standing on familiar ground. Her need to identify her standing—was this just a coupling that wouldn't be significant a month from now or a budding relationship they'd still treasure years from now? The question that always seemed to rear its ugly head at the wrong moment.

She sat up, putting enough distance between them to allow herself to think without emotion. "No, I don't need a label. I'm one of those girls who likes to know what's going on. To make sure I'm aware. Through the lens of a camera, you see things others might overlook. I don't overlook anything. I can't afford to."

"What do you want me to say? I don't have a clue."

She pressed her lips together. There was no way she'd spill her feelings or let him know what she felt for him in such a short period. She wasn't some pathetic woman who was so desperate for a companion that she'd let herself think she'd fallen in love with a man she hardly knew. She shook the thoughts away so he couldn't read anything on her face.

Another crash in some part of the house made her scramble to her knees. Xander was on his feet like a cat with nine lives. Before she could stand, he'd slipped his cargo shorts on over his bare butt.

She pulled on her panties and reached for her tank and skirt.

"It's probably just another limb, right?" She didn't sound convincing even to herself.

"Not a chance I want to take." He reached for the Glock on the bar and shoved it into his waistband. "You know the drill."

"Give me a minute. I need to put on my top. I'll feel less vulnerable."

"You have a Glock. You're not vulnerable."

She pulled her tank over her head. "I should put on my sandals."

"Olivia, focus." He gripped her shoulders. "You're going to be okay. I'll check out what's going on. You stay here."

He didn't let her go until she said yes. Then he inched toward the door without taking his eyes off her.

"Okay, okay." She tried to smile convincingly.

He opened the door. Two sumo-sized guys on the other side pushed it the rest of the way. They were on him before she drew the gun.

CHAPTER 24

*I*f he'd been paying attention when he opened the door, there was no way Godzilla could have taken out his knees while King Kong crushed his jaw with a punch so hard it could have taken down the Empire State building.

Olivia's scream had echoed in his head, like an unending siren. But no one could scream that long without taking a breath. It was impossible.

Then everything went black.

A pain radiated through his body, moving from one limb to the next then up his spine. If he could move to another position, maybe it would go away. His body refused to cooperate. His arms worked against his legs, and neither of them was successful. He needed to remember something important, but what? He was heavy—as if a weight hung from every extremity. Breathing required more than the usual effortless in-and-out. He wanted to curl into a ball and sleep for a while, but something in the back of his brain nudged him to open his eyes.

Every cell in his body ached. The pain from his head radiated down his neck into his shoulders before continuing to his fingernails. Everything was fuzzy around the edges. No matter how hard he tried, he couldn't clear his head or organize more than one thought at a time. His body was out of synch. The pounding in his head didn't match the throbbing of his heart or the all-over ache.

He was on the floor, crumpled against the wall of the media room. He knew the location because it was the only carpeted floor in his house and the sound of Al Pacino raging in *Scarface* played on the screen. Based on the movie, maybe an hour had passed.

He needed to do something. If he could open his eyes, then maybe he could remember.

He lay motionless. He had to pull his thoughts together.

Olivia Sika. The bronze beauty pulled him out of the stupor, forcing him to recall everything.

Was Olivia here in the room? Opening his eyes shouldn't have been so hard. It was something he'd done millions of times without thought, but he couldn't do it now. Something warm ran down his face toward his mouth. He stuck out his tongue and licked his lips.

Blood.

His blood, no doubt.

He tried to sit up, but he slipped and fell hard back to the floor. His hands were taped, and so were his feet, but at least he was alive.

Was Olivia okay? He'd be fine, of that he was sure. This little incident wasn't the first time someone had tried to take him out by hitting him on the head. They must not have gotten the message from his mother, that his head was as hard as his ass.

With a sudden jerk, his third attempt to sit up was successful. He drew in a deep breath. With his head resting against the wall, the blood flowed down his cheek. His head throbbed in unison with his heartbeat. This helplessness wasn't going to solve this problem. Only he could do that.

He tried again to open his eyes and managed the simple task. Instead of seeing the sharp edges he was used to, everything was fuzzy and shadowy. He narrowed his focus to the legs of the barstool. The oak legs came into perfect view. So did the satchel of ammo. It was still in the corner. He shifted his head. A shooting pain ricocheted across his skull. He closed his eyes, processing the pain into manageable pieces.

When the spasm subsided enough, he opened his eyes again, fighting through the blinding pain. He had to know where Olivia was. Without moving his head, he scanned the room. She wasn't in sight. The Glock he'd given her earlier wasn't on the bar either.

He groaned. His head restricted his ability to take in enough air, but he had no option. It was time to find Olivia and to figure out what was going on.

CHAPTER 25

One of the men seemed to take the orders, not give them. He shoved Olivia onto the bed, in what was probably Xander's bedroom, and then he snatched the phone cord out of the outlet and wrapped it around his thick arm.

Olivia examined their faces. Nothing about either of them was familiar, and nothing resembled the images she'd developed of the man stalking her.

"We won't have to worry about her," Brute-Number-One said. He was the one who had landed the blow to Xander's head and had grabbed her while Brute-Number-Two had wrapped duct tape around Xander's wrist and ankles.

"Don't do anything stupid. I'd hate to mess up that pretty face." The biggest one said before they walked out and closed the door. Fear froze her in place. The attack had left Xander bleeding into the carpet. There was a lot of blood. Nothing made sense. Whoever the stalker was, he had her now. Wasn't that the goal? Why were they hanging around?

She took deep breaths trying to slow her heart rate long enough to put two coherent thoughts together. "One. Two. Three. Four. Five," she whispered. She needed to calm down.

Panicking wouldn't help Xander. The way he'd crumbled to the floor said he was going to need help. And soon. He was unconscious and bleeding on the floor like trash.

From somewhere in the house a mumbled conversation filtered into the room. Trying to decipher the words was impossible. She eased her body onto the soft mattress and stared at the ceiling. Stalking wasn't a group activity, so why were there two men just beyond the bedroom door? Now that Xander wasn't a threat, why hadn't her stalker fled the premise with her in tow? Something wasn't adding up.

She wrung her hand. Xander had to be okay. If not for her, he wouldn't be in the middle of a hurricane with a busted head.

"Think, Olivia, think." She thumped her forehead. What was going on here? If her stalker wanted to kill her, he could have done that so much easier in New York.

She couldn't help worrying about Xander. He might not even be alive. The thought strangled her breath in her throat.

The wind wasn't battering the house with the same gusto as before, but the rain hadn't lightened up any.

Without knocking, one of the men opened the door. She studied the face of Brute-Number-Two. Should she know him? She didn't recognize him, and she'd like to think she'd remember all her clients. Had she stepped on his toe on the subway or scorned him on one of her forgettable blind dates? Nothing about him was familiar. He was an average white man, but with enough extra weight to slow him down. All he needed was some green shading, and he could be the Hulk's twin.

"Ever heard of knocking? What, you guys don't have any manners?" She soaked her words with sarcasm.

"This ain't no bed and breakfast."

"Why did you have to hit Xander so hard? You probably

broke his leg and cracked his skull. You want me—now you've got me, leave him alone."

He didn't respond. Instead, he stared at her with cold, empty eyes.

"Is he okay? His head was bleeding."

"You ask a lot of questions. Maybe I should tape your mouth shut."

She sat up. "Do I know you or the other asshole you're with?"

"Doesn't matter."

"Do you know me?"

He leaned against the door opening. His belly hung over his pants. "Like I said, doesn't matter."

"Aren't you supposed to hide your face?"

"Honey, you won't see me again after today."

She folded her arms over her chest. "Promises, promises." She muttered. "I need my pain pills for my knee. After you ran me off the road, I twisted it."

"We'll see about that."

"You're admitting to running me off the road."

"I'm not saying anything. I wish you'd shut the hell up. I don't want to hit a woman." He folded his arms over his chest.

"What do you guys want? If it's me, why can't you leave Xander alone?"

"I want you to stop asking questions." He spoke without looking at her. His attention was focus towards the kitchen.

"Then start answering them."

He turned to face her. "Honey, you need to learn the world doesn't revolve around you. By now you should see, I'm calling the shots, not you and not your boyfriend."

"Xander is not my boyfriend."

"He ought to be the way the two of you have been going at it." His wicked grin made her angrier.

"You're a peeping tom?"

"Stop talking to her." The voice from the other room sounded rough and even more threatening. "…and get back in here, he wants to talk to us."

"I'll be back for you." He pointed his tattooed index finger at her.

"I can't wait." She turned her back to him before he closed the door.

CHAPTER 26

*T*rying to call for help wouldn't accomplish anything, and it would only let anyone left in the house know he was awake. Xander shimmied across the floor, trying to get closer to his bag of ammo. Movement was almost impossible with his hands and feet taped together. Every time he moved, his head reminded him not to. He stopped. For several moments he was perfectly still. He had to get free, to find Olivia. He'd made too many promises not to keep them.

Something hard in his pocket pressed into his thigh.

His blade!

He snapped his head up and tried to ignore the pain searing through him. The numbskulls hadn't even bothered to search him. He maneuvered himself onto his opposite side. His first attempt to free the cutter wasn't successful. He flattened his back against the floor, and with his index finger, flipped up the flap on his pocket and slid his fingers inside. He managed to grab the blade, but then it slipped out. His head thunked against the wall. Even if he got the knife, how could he cut the tape around his wrist?

He looked around the room. Something caught his attention. Glinting like the pot of gold at the end of a rainbow was a shard of glass. All he had to do was move ten feet.

Olivia needed him. Making sure she was okay was the only thing that mattered, not the pain in his head, not the blood running down his face, nothing. He used the wall as leverage to cross the room, pushing his shoulder blades hard against the wall. The movement was slow, but it worked. Blood continued to flow, covering his eye. He used his shoulder to wipe the blood off his cheek before continuing.

He reached the piece of glass and paused long enough to wince from the pain. He positioned the glass on its end between his palms then, rubbed his wrist across the glass several times. The slow back and forth process would take too long. He nicked the heels of his palms several times on the sharp edge.

The tape gave way, but now his palms bled as much as his head injury. With his hands free, he pulled the knife from his pocket and snipped the tape binding his feet. He reached for his shirt, tore off two strips and tied them on his wrist, covering his cuts.

Without hesitating, he opened the bag containing his arsenal and removed the semi-automatic assault weapon and loaded the magazine. Next, he pulled out the Beretta, loaded bullets into the chamber, and shoved it into the pocket of his shorts.

There were at least two of them. He had enough ammo to take care of ten.

CHAPTER 27

Olivia sat up and tried to hear the conversation in the other room. Something wasn't going the way they had expected. The two idiots in the kitchen were talking louder. She climbed off the bed and tried the doorknob. Even though the door locked from the inside, she couldn't open it. She yanked the handle again with more force this time this time, and it gave way.

The heated argument in the kitchen continued. The two men stood near the sink.

"Who the hell changes a plan mid-way?"

"You can ask him when he gets here. He's the boss of the operation, we just take orders."

Without waiting to hear more, Olivia closed the door and moved along the wall toward the media room. She had to find Xander. He had to be okay.

She hurried toward the media room. The voices in the kitchen weren't as loud as they were a few seconds ago.

Her heart thundered in her chest, but fear didn't slow her down. Xander needed her help. She rounded the corner and smacked into him.

"Are you okay?" She threw her arms around his neck, careful to avoid the weapon in his hand. Blood streaked down his face. His ripped shirt was saturated with blood on the side where the butt of the gun had struck his head. She kissed his cheek, his chin, and his lips, before squeezing him tight, careful not to touch the gash along his temple.

He peeled away and looked at her. "Did they hurt you?"

"No, but look at your head. What happened to your hands?"

He ignored her.

She reached up to touch the knot blooming on his forehead, but he drew away. "Do you recognize either one of them?"

"No."

He stared into her eyes for a moment as if her answer wasn't believable.

"Where are they now?"

"In the kitchen. I overheard them talking. They're waiting for someone else to get here. Someone who's going to change the plan."

"What plan?

"I don't know. I couldn't hear everything."

"How many are there?"

"I only saw two."

"How many weapons?"

"I don't know. They did grab the Glock off the bar in the media room after they hit you." She shrugged. "I only talked to one of them. If he had another gun, he's hiding it."

The lights flickered, then the house went dark.

"We just lost power. Go to the media room and lock the door." He pointed down the hall.

"No. I'm going with you. Because of me, they've hurt you." She couldn't keep waiting for someone else to solve her problem. If she couldn't step up now, she deserved whatever happened next.

"I don't have time to argue with you, Olivia. Please stay here."

"I'm not arguing, Xander. Give me a gun. I'm going with you." The determination in her voice didn't leave room for him to argue it out.

He pulled a gun from his pants pocket that was smaller than the Glock he'd given her earlier.

"Hey, she's gone." The voice rang through the house, followed by the sound of running footsteps.

Xander shoved her behind him and lifted the assault rifle. With the footsteps of a panther, he made his way toward the front of the house and signaled for her to follow. Before stepping into the main hall opening, he held up his hand.

She stopped.

The husky man who had stood in Xander's bedroom doorway lumbered around the corner like a washed-up-sprinter. Xander fired his weapon. Two rapid shots and he dropped to the floor, cradling his knees. His buddy was so close behind he didn't have a moment to adjust to the situation. Xander dropped him, too, with one bullet in the shoulder that sent him backward. He managed to hold on to his gun and got off a wild shot that went into the ceiling above his head.

Xander moved toward them with a swiftness she'd only seen in animals. He kicked one gun away, sending it across the living room and under the sofa and wrangled the second gun out of the hand of Brute-Number-Two before he could regroup.

The big one continued to hold his knees. "Fuck man," he whined.

"Do me a favor, gentlemen, please don't bleed all over my floor. I don't mind cleaning up after myself, but I hate it when uninvited people show up at my place and make a mess." He turned to Olivia. "There is tape in the kitchen, on the pantry floor," he said with the gun pointed at the head of Brute-Number-One. "Get it for me, and let's take care of these two."

She returned to find him in the same position, with a look on his face she didn't ever need to see again. There were three cell phones and two pistols in a pile several feet away that had to have belonged to these guys. Xander had slipped into professional mode. His movements were exact and efficient. He scrolled through the phones and emptied the bullets from both guns as if this was a routine task.

He made her feel safe. What would happen to whoever was supposed to show up next?

"Who are you waiting for?" Xander asked after binding the hands and feet of both men with such precision it would take Harry Houdini to set them free.

Both men kept their heads down.

"So, you two assholes are following directions from someone with a brain just a wee bigger than yours. Why does he want Olivia?"

"Who the hell is Olivia?" Brute-Number-Two spat out.

Xander's head snapped up. His eyes met hers.

CHAPTER 28

*X*ander couldn't put words to the surge racing through his body. These two shit-heads didn't know the difference between a peach and a pear, so he couldn't make anything of the fact that they didn't know Olivia. They were only following orders.

"Olivia, go down to the media room and hit the light switches. Make sure they're off. The generator kicked on."

"There's no power, of course, the lights are off."

"Just in case the electricity comes back on, I want the house dark."

She nodded before going down the hall.

Both men bled onto his pristine bamboo floors, but if that meant Olivia's ordeal would be over shortly, then it was worth the price.

She came back and said, "Okay, what else can I do?"

"Go into the kitchen and see if you can find our cell phones. Check those light switches, too."

She headed off.

"Oh yeah, see if you can find your Glock!" he yelled.

Less than two minutes later she was back. "Here's your

cell. I found mine and the Glock." She held up her yellow phone case. "Here, let me wipe some of that blood off your face."

She pressed a towel to his temple and forehead with dabbing motions. Her touch was tentative, moving from one spot to the next.

He grabbed her hand. "I'm fine for now."

He dialed Omar. "I need you. Stake out my house. If you see a car make the turn toward the beach, call me immediately. I'm expecting an unwanted visitor."

"You know we're in the middle of a hurricane, don't you?" Omar protested.

"This is business. I'll fill you in on the details once you get in place. Bring the backup and call Jimmie. Tell him I need him here with the squad car."

"It might take Jimmie a while to get there, but I'm on my way." Omar ended the call.

"We might as well get comfortable." He handed her the AR-15. "Hold this for me, and if one of these thugs moves an iota, put a bullet in his empty head."

He checked their pockets and socks and shoes to make sure there were no hidden weapons. These two weren't going anywhere.

He grabbed Olivia by the hand and guided her across the room to the sofa. "These two don't know you, and you don't know them. That means there is more going on than what we think."

"I've been turning over the same rocks, and I haven't found an answer."

He pulled his phone from his pocket. "We'll see what happens when the other one arrives. He's got to be the one."

She smacked her cell in her palm while staring at the floor. She looked like she was processing the same thoughts that kept poking at him. How did all these pieces fit together? He had to solve this mystery if he ever wanted to see that sparkle in her eye that he'd first witnessed at the airport.

His phone rang. "Omar, talk to me."

"I'm in place. The storm has died down, and the rain is much lighter. What the hell is going on over there?"

Xander gave him the details.

"You've got two dudes tied up on your floor right now?"

"Sure do. Now we're just waiting for one more to show up. I'm guessing he's the stalker."

"Well, your wish is getting ready to come true. A big black limousine just made the turn down your hill."

"A limousine? I guess he's not trying to hide his appearance. Get the tag number and follow him in. Have the guys flank the house on all sides. Just don't let him see you. Text me if you can get an idea of how many people are in the car."

"I know the routine. Let's get prepared for some fireworks." The eagerness in Omar's voice said he was ready for what they did best.

CHAPTER 29

Olivia paced the length of the room, avoiding eye contact with the men on the floor. While Xander was wide-eyed with excitement like a child at a mega birthday party, her nerves were frayed. If she were a nail-biter, she'd be down to nubs by now.

"What's happening?" Her voice shook as much as her hands.

"We're getting ready to have some company," Xander spoke low. He checked the chambers of his weapons. "You've got your Glock?"

She nodded.

He placed his hand on her leg. "Look at me, Olivia. I know you want to be a part of this, and I understand why, but this is what I do, and I'm damn good at it. I'm going to need you to listen to me and do what I say." He spoke slow, emphasizing each word.

"Xander, don't ask me to—"

"Olivia, listen to me." He increased the pressure on her leg. "I can't put you in danger. I just can't."

"But you're hurt. I can help. Let's call the police—your friend, Jimmie."

"Omar has notified Jimmie. Besides, I'm fine. And I'll be even better if I don't have to worry about you. Nobody is going to get to you unless I'm dead. And if I am dead, I want you to use the Glock. Keep shooting until it's empty."

She wanted to say something, but nothing would be good enough. No one had ever risked his life for her. The thought was exhilarating and heartbreaking at the same time. Could she lose Xander just when they were discovering something new?

Xander shook her away from her thoughts. "I want you to go into the master bedroom. Lock the door and push something in front of it. Stay in there until I come for you. If you must go out the French doors, take the stairs on the south side of the deck and make your way up the main road. Don't look back, just run like hell. One of my guys will be there for you."

Tears stung her eyes. "You'll come, won't you Xander? Promise me."

He grabbed her shoulders and pulled her forward. The kiss he gave her was the most tender connection she'd ever experienced. It was as if he gave her his soul—handing it over for safe keeping. "I promise. You are my only priority right now." He peered into her eyes for several seconds. "Now you've got to go, baby."

She bit her bottom lip and then made her way toward the bedroom. With a quick look back at Xander, her heart swelled.

He blew her a kiss.

In the bedroom, she followed his instructions, pushing both nightstands against the door. They wouldn't keep out anyone who was intent on getting to her out, but it would slow them down. She sat on the edge of the bed with the gun in her hand.

Her heart wouldn't slow down. She tried to control her breathing, but how could she calm down with so much going on? She fingered the thin fabric of her skirt. There was no way she could run from anyone in a garment down to her ankles. She grabbed hold of the slit and ripped the material, leaving behind a zig-zag hemline above her knees.

Now she was ready for battle.

CHAPTER 30

*X*ander kept his eye on the limousine as it pulled into his drive. Something wasn't adding up. This wasn't the first time he'd dealt with stalkers, and nothing about this one was by the book. Stalkers operated alone. They didn't enlist aides to help them intimidate their victims. Where was the pleasure in that?

Both passenger side doors opened and out stepped two more barbarians dressed in black suits and ties with white shirts. They could have been extras from a bad Eighties' movie. The bulk of their jackets did little to hide the fact they were packing. Their appearance posed more questions.

Xander pulled one of the intruders he'd shot in the shoulder to his feet. "Since you don't want to talk, you'll make an excellent shield."

The guy tried to jerk away, but Xander held him tight. With his arm around the guy's throat, he pushed him toward the door and then opened it. He pointed the AR-15 at the new arrivals his drive. "I don't like visitors who show up at my place without an invitation," he said.

Jacob Popov stepped out of the limousine and adjusted

his tie. What the hell was Jacob doing here? He'd been clear with Jacob that he didn't want his business. Jacob's intimidation tactics made Xander's trigger finger itch.

Jacob adjusted his tie. "That's no way to talk to someone who's come all this way in a hurricane to do business with you." If the small yard wasn't cluttered in tree debris, and two men hadn't invaded his home, and his heart wasn't racing, and Olivia wasn't locked up in his bedroom, Jacob's tone would have sounded like it was an ordinary day and this was an ordinary visit.

Jacob was persistent. Which only meant one thing. Xander was right to turn down his business. If Jacob needed traditional surveillance on a traditional warehouse, he wouldn't have taken these extreme measures. Jacob was trafficking something and need more muscle than his street thugs provided.

Xander pointed the shaft on the gun at his visitor. "I should have known you were behind this, Jacob."

The two bodyguards drew their weapons. Jacob signaled for them to relax before sauntering toward the house. "You didn't think I was going to take no for an answer, did you? You must not have done your homework."

"Stay right there, Jacob. My homework is the reason I said no. And no amount of bullying is going to make me change my mind. I think you're the one who hasn't done his homework or you would have known that."

Jacob had a swagger that was matched only by his sense of entitlement. Even now, he didn't hesitate as he took another step forward as if he were invited over for cocktails. The scar across his cheek hinted at the kind of life he lived, the life that he couldn't hide behind fancy clothes, big cars, and piles of cash. Xander had run into guys like Jacob, before but never had one been so persistent.

"Did you enjoy the visit from the two gentlemen I sent by earlier today to get you ready for our discussion?"

"Oh, I got them ready for the discussion," he said. "Your thugs may need to stop by a doctor before they stop by the police station." Xander pressed his finger into the wound of the man shielding him. The cry that came from the guy's throat echoed in the wind.

The slight lift of Jacob's eyebrow was the only emotion he showed. "Can we go inside and talk business?" Jacob made another move forward.

Xander aimed the gun at Jacob's chest. "I wouldn't come any closer if I were you. I'm not having any visitors today, and as I told you, we have nothing to discuss. And just in case you don't know, you're not the only one who has tactics to handle asshole clients. Do yourself a favor and forget my number. You'll wish you had." The tone of his voice left no room for discussion.

Neither did the weapon he pointed at Jacob's head.

"What about my men?"

"Oh, they broke into my house and clocked me on the head. They aren't going to get away with that. If they implicated you as the person who sent them, then that's something you'll have to work out with the police." He waved the gun back at the limousine. "Now you'd better go, or all of you will end up like the two inside."

"Now, Mr. Fitzgerald you must not be aware of my capabilities." Jacob looked over his shoulder. "I intend to have my way. It's three against one."

Xander nodded toward the yard and signaled for Omar. From the shadows, Omar and five guys stepped out. Each of them with an AR-15 trained on Jacob and his men.

Jacob pointed at Xander. "We're not done, Fitzgerald."

"You better hope this is the last time I see your ugly mug because the next time I promise you I won't be this hospitable. Now get your stinking ass off my property. I have an escort for you."

Jimmie pulled the squad car along the road and made his way up the drive. "You got a problem here, Xander?"

Jacob made his way to his car and climbed inside. The two thugs followed him without looking up.

"I've got this one and another one in the house. You can take them with you. They both need medical attention. And you'll want to talk to the head asshole in that car." Xander pointed to the limousine pulling away. I'll come down to the station and fill out the reports," Xander said.

"Looks like you solved your mystery." Jimmie hiked up his cargo shorts and headed inside.

"No, I don't think we have."

CHAPTER 31

*O*livia scanned the beach before pulling the visor down over her forehead. The sun was back in full force. With no remnants of the hurricane visible on the beach, she could almost make herself believe it was just a dream. The weather on the island may be as fickle as a woman, but there was nothing unsteady about her feelings for Xander. He was everything she wanted—strong, honest, gentle, and excellent in bed. Plus, he came with a whole list of extras she hadn't even known she'd wanted, like being good-looking, having a sense of humor, and being able to carry her. But he lived on Sebastian Island, and she lived in New York. That wasn't a long-distance relationship; that was a relationship death knell. Sure, she'd make that choice for the perfect man. There was only one big stumbling block. Xander hadn't extended an offer.

The marmalade sun warmed her skin, and she pushed away thoughts of her stay on the island coming to an end. Her stalker issue wasn't resolved. David had nothing new to report. Without her presence in New York, her stalker didn't have a reason to taunt her.

Xander flipped over in his beach chair to face her. "What would you like to do tonight?" His skin glowed with the generous dose of suntan lotion he'd applied.

"I hope I'm going to meet with the African artist later this evening, and then I must start making arrangements to get back to New York. *Beauty Bar* loved the spread I just completed for them, and they're thinking about doing something on location, so I want to be there to nudge them in my direction."

"If you don't mind, I'd like to tag along this evening. We can do something afterward."

She picked up her camera and snapped several pictures of him. The goal was to catch him in every mood, in different lights, and with several expressions, so when she got home, she had a tangible way to remember him. He opened his eye unusually large for one shot, and then he curled his lips sideways for another.

"I love it when you act goofy." She put the camera down.

"What do you mean goofy? Those faces were supposed to be eye-catching." He climbed out of his chair to stand above her. "How about later today? Are you going to take me up on my offer?"

"Yeah. Sounds like a good idea."

He bent over and held her face in his hands. "I don't know if I said this before, but you are a gorgeous woman." He held out his hand to her.

She stood. "Thanks." What else could she say? What she wanted to hear was, *can you stay longer, what's going to happen between us after this vacation is over, or even better, I'm in love with you.*

She cocked her head to the side. By now she should have had a better understanding of life—expect the unexpected. Or not expecting anything at all. At least that way, there was no disappointment.

"We'd better get changed. I'm supposed to meet the artist at seven." She made her way to her place. They were staying in her rental while his house was undergoing repairs and clean-up. She didn't need to see some of those reminders. Even though the events of the last few days had energized Xander, they'd left her drained. He seemed anxious to get on to his next assignment.

She dropped her bag inside the door. "That's my phone ringing." She fished it from her bag. "David, I was hoping you'd call. Have you found out anything?" She sat on the edge of the kitchen chair.

"Nothing, Olivia. I'm sorry," David said.

"Don't be, you tried."

"I'm not giving up. We'll find this jerk," His apologetic tone tugged at her heart.

This trip had both good moments and bad moments. It was difficult to know what to feel. Life back in New York would require the same cautious steps as before, but the thought of leaving Xander was the hardest thing of all to face.

CHAPTER 32

*X*ander held the gift shop door open for Olivia. The *ding* of the bell signaled their arrival. Several customers milled around the small space. There was a large selection of cheap souvenirs cluttering the shelves at the front of the store. The colorful display was for tourists in search of inexpensive trinkets to take home to remember their stay on Sebastian. Olivia headed straight for the register where a short line of customers waited to pay for their goods. The attractive shop owner wore a colorful African print turban around her head. She moved with the gracefulness of a gazelle and almost as fast.

He'd made a promise to find her stalker—a promise he hadn't kept. Few things rattled him more than an incomplete job or an unhappy client. She wasn't asking for much, just to be able to live a normal life, open a door without being spooked. And he'd thought they were close to finding her stalker, but instead of nailing her stalker, the ordeal had been all about him. The failure sat on his chest like Mount Olympus.

"Is he here, the artist?" Olivia's voice was as familiar his own now, and she sounded happy.

"Yes, Isoke is here. I told him about you. I'd hoped you'd come back to the shop. He's in the back." She led them to the rear of the store where the more expensive collectors' items adorned the glass cases.

Olivia's taste ran toward eclectic. His taste centered on modern. But he understood her need to grasp her history and wanting to surround herself with its richness. One thing he'd learned about the two of them was while they burned up the sheets in every way imaginable, they were opposites when it came to other areas of their lives. Crossing from one world to the other would take more than desire, and there were no guarantees either of them wanted it enough to take the chance. He couldn't make the mistake of moving too fast again. The skid marks from Hope remained imprinted on his heart.

She'd been very quiet the last few days. Even though he wanted to think it was because of the incident with Jacob, his instincts told him that wasn't the only reason. She had to be disappointed too, in the way things turned out.

"Isoke, this is the woman I told you about," said the shop owner. "I'm sorry. I don't know your name." She turned to Olivia.

After Olivia introduced them both, she smiled. Her face brightened enough to almost match her yellow sundress. Too bad he wasn't the one to bring her that kind of joy.

"How did you recognize my work?" Isoke asked. His heavy African accent made him hard to understand.

"I can't say I know your work personally—but I love it. I was in Benin, and I saw similar pieces."

Isoke nodded. "I can show you more. Some pieces I'm working on are in the corner." He nodded over his shoulder to a collection of statues in shades of brown and canvas, with abstracts in dazzling shades of oranges and yellows. No wonder she was drawn to his work.

She clapped her hands as if he'd just told her she'd won the lottery.

"Go ahead," Xander said. "I need to call Omar to discuss some business. I'll be right outside."

Putting a little distance between them was like taking off a sweater that was too tight. Olivia was different, he knew why, but there was nothing he could do about that right now. He needed more time.

Outside the shop, the breeze wasn't forceful enough to shake away his doubt or make him feel any better. He pulled his phone from his pocket and dialed Omar. "Any luck tracking that information from her phone? It's been a week."

"Yeah, well whoever sent those messages to Olivia didn't want us to find him. I need a little more time. I can tell you they came from New York. Give me a day or two, and I'll narrow it down more."

"She's leaving tomorrow. How can I be her hero if I can't solve this mystery for her before she leaves?"

"I'm doing the best I can, boss. Give me two days, tops. If you want to sit behind a computer with me, we might be able to speed this up." The sound of Omar striking the computer keys came through the phone.

"Maybe tomorrow after her flight. I'll need something mind-numbing to occupy my thoughts. See you then." He ended the call and re-entered the store just in time to see Olivia coming out of the back room with another large wood carving. Isoke was able to make her smile. A big one.

"Look at this. Isn't it beautiful? I've got to figure out how I'm going to get this home." She sounded happy.

"After your flight tomorrow, I'll have it packaged and sent to you."

She nodded. "Now you must feed me. I'm starved."

He hooked his arm through hers and led her toward the row of restaurants, wanting to cherish the remaining moments with her.

There were just a few things he needed to remember: first, don't ask her to come live in Sebastian. Second, he couldn't make a fool of himself talking about love and tomorrows. And third, no matter what, don't ask Olivia to marry him.

CHAPTER 33

Olivia let Xander hold her carving and accepted his arm. Romanticizing about the past week would have been her go-to response, but it was going to be hard enough to leave him. There was no use in dwelling on what could have been. Other than the hurricane, the bike accident, and being held captive for an hour or two, the week could not have been better even if one of those love-story television networks had written the script.

The only thing that could explain why she was out-of-sorts was the same thing that always tripped her up. Her expectations. Her mother often said Olivia was never satisfied, and at this moment that was the truth.

"Can we just walk around downtown this evening? I don't want to spend my last few hours on the island cooped up in a restaurant, staring out the window," she said.

"We can do whatever you want." Xander squeezed her hand. "This is Olde Towne. The island was settled in the sixteen hundreds and was a great hideout for pirates."

"How do you know so much?"

PICTURES FROM PARADISE | 151

"I live here now. I enjoy sitting in the small coffee shops talking to the locals. This island is pretty perfect. Come back for another visit soon, and I promise there won't be any incidents to disrupt your stay."

She slowed her pace. "Is that the only thing you can promise me?"

"I also promise to make sure none of my clients do anything to torture you."

She studied his face, looking for some telltale sign that he didn't want her to go. That maybe he was feeling something for her, too.

But, there wasn't one. This was the pattern in her life. She attracted the weirdos and the handsome guys with desirable traits who gave her plenty of compliments, but seldom anything else.

"Hey, if you haven't tasted our Belgium waffle ice cream sandwiches, then you have to before you leave." He released her arm to grab her hand. Together, they crossed the street and made their way to the pink-and-green awning with the words *frozen treats* scripted on the front.

Xander ordered for both of them while she sat at the small round table positioned under the shade of the awning. Within minutes, he took the seat next to her.

"This thing is huge. We could have shared one," she said after taking her first bite.

"You say that now. But when you're halfway through, you're going to want the whole thing and maybe a piece of mine."

"You know, Xander." She placed her elbow on the table. "I thought we had something pretty special."

His eyes darkened. "We did." His voice was stiff, expecting.

"I guess what I'm trying to say is, I'm a little surprised you haven't asked me to stay or offered to come to New York or talked about what's next for us."

He placed his ice cream sandwich on the napkin and rubbed his hands together, then exhaled. "Olivia, I hope I haven't misled you. I'm not interested in a long-term relationship. I was in one a few years ago, and I promised myself I wouldn't go back into one anytime soon. If I wasn't clear about my feelings, then I'm sorry. I'd love to see you again, but I'm not ready to get serious. I don't know when I will be." He reached for her hand.

She pulled away. There was no way she was going to cry. She was a big girl. This wasn't the first time she didn't get what she wanted, but this was one of the most heartbreaking.

She sat up straight and reached for her cheery voice. "Sure, I understand. Maybe it's was the sound of the ocean and the beautiful sunsets that made me get carried away." She forced a smile onto her face. "I hope I didn't put you in an awkward situation."

He leaned toward her, placing both his hands on the sides of her face. "I can say that, if I *were* going to fall for anyone, then you'd be the one."

"Yeah, me, too." She put her ice cream sandwich on top of his and stood. "I think we should head back now. I'll need to get packed. My flight is out early in the morning."

The ride back to the beach was unusually quiet. At the entrance to her rental, he leaned against the door. "Don't you want some company your last night on the island?" Xander had the sincerest look on his face. His eyes spoke to her in a way his words in town hadn't.

She kissed his cheek. "Xander, you've made this trip unforgettable, and for that, I'll always be thankful, but I think I need to be alone tonight."

His facial expression shifted. "Oh. All right." He straightened. "I'll come down early in the morning to get you to the airport."

She nodded, but she couldn't afford to ignore the statement he'd made in town. As much as her heart wanted to think she could change his mind, or that one day, he'd fall madly in love with her, she had to live her life using her head. Her life and her future depended on it.

CHAPTER 34

Olivia opened the door to her Queens apartment with a heaviness that was sure to linger for weeks. Sure, she'd been on vacation, but the weight around her neck when she left was still around her neck. Now there was a different label on the weight. Xander's name was written all over it. Considering everything that had happened, the stalker seemed almost insignificant.

Eva had picked her up at JFK. The ride home had been a quiet one.

"See? Your apartment is as good as new. David and I made sure of it." Eva was more bubbly than usual.

"Thank you, Eva. You guys are like gold to me. And thanks for getting the locks changed. I'll be much more selective about who gets a key this time." Oliva placed her camera bag on the kitchen counter.

"Okay, girl, dish. Something happened in Sebastian. Your face is as long as a New York winter."

Olivia shrugged. "There isn't a lot to tell. I thought Xander and I were building something, but, like before, I was wrong."

Eva rubbed her back. The action reeked with sympathy. "I'm so sorry. But maybe you're looking at it the wrong way. You had a fling. Everyone needs a good fling to flush out the cobwebs sometimes."

"I can always count on you to find a bright side."

"Wait and see if he calls you in a few days."

"Eva, this morning I called a cab two hours earlier than I needed to so I wasn't there when Xander came to take me to the airport. I wanted to get through security so I wouldn't have to see him." She flopped onto the sofa. "For me, there was a period at the end of the Xander sentence. What I need to focus on now is who has been running my life. That and my job are going to be where I put my focus."

Eva tilted her head. The weak smile said all the things Eva was too polite to say. She might not agree with Olivia's new direction, but, like any good friend, she said nothing.

Neither of them spoke for several seconds. Olivia couldn't help but wonder what Xander thought when he'd knocked on the rental door and found her gone. Maybe she was wrong for just leaving, but she had to protect her heart.

"So now what?" Eva asked.

"I'm back in the studio tomorrow. Ajay and Gwen have texted me and both are ready to go. I may even get another gig from *Beauty Bar*. So far, they like my proposal. My life will go on without Xander, it just won't be as glossy."

CHAPTER 35

*X*ander settled lower in the chair, mimicking the sun as it dropped below the horizon. Olivia's leaving wasn't supposed to impact him. Why she felt the need to slip away without letting him know was something only she knew. He wasn't a monster.

He examined his cell phone. After dialing her number several times, she wasn't picking up. He couldn't blame her. He'd have to be a complete moron not to know she wanted more from him, but he couldn't, not right now. The promises he'd made to himself were valid for good reasons. The next time he strolled down Lover's Lane he had to be sure.

His mother's favorite saying was that things work out for the best, and in this case, he had to hope his mother was right. Olivia would probably always see him as the man who didn't solve her most pressing problem. And she'd be right.

His ego couldn't handle that.

The phone vibrated in his hand. He glanced at the screen before accepting the call. "Yeah, Omar."

"I thought you were going to stop in. Two hands would

make this whole process go faster. Don't you want to find out who's has been stalking Olivia?"

What he wanted to do was sulk a little longer. He was supposed to be the one living on the edge. Staring down challenges without blinking, but mustering the energy seemed impossible.

He heaved his body out of the chair. Tracking the data from Olivia's phone would give him something to focus his attention on. "I'm on my way." He walked out the door. How much longer would he glance down the slope and wish Olivia was standing on the deck?

Omar lived in town. Growing up on an island, he'd grown weary of the water and sand years ago. An hour after Omar's call, Xander balanced a carton of peas and rice in one hand and rang Omar's doorbell with the other.

Omar opened the door. "I was beginning to think you weren't going to show. Since Olivia left this morning, I thought you'd moved on to your next conquest."

"Just so you know, I bought us a snack." Xander held up the brown paper bag. "And I don't do conquests. Not anymore. Haven't you noticed that I'm more thoughtful about my relationships now?"

Omar led the way inside. "I can't say I see any difference. Since Hope, you've taken your love life underground."

He followed Omar. "No, I haven't. That's just it. I'm not dating."

"You and Olivia looked very familiar."

Xander pushed the papers covering the table aside and set the food down. "How are you making out with the search?"

"Ah, you're changing the subject, so that means I was right."

Xander stared at his assistant. There were two ways to go, lie or tell the truth. Lying wouldn't do Olivia justice, and he couldn't bring himself to say anything about her that wasn't true. "She left this morning without waiting for me to take her to the airport."

"What did you do to screw things up?" Omar pulled plates and forks from the cabinet, then handed one of each to Xander.

"I told her the truth. I'm not ready to get serious."

"That's your problem. Why do you think you always need to be honest with women? They don't want honesty. They want the dream. Give them what they want."

"That's not my style. Not anymore. After the way Hope dumped me, I'm always going to tell the women in my life the truth."

"There won't be any women in your life if that's your philosophy."

"Like I'm going to take advice from you." Xander sat and spooned out some food onto his plate. "That's enough talk about my love life. Let's get to work."

Omar wolfed down his food—the way he always did— then pushed his plate aside. He turned the computer around to give Xander a clear view of the screen. "Take a look at this. I have thirty messages here that I was able to track to the same cell tower in Queens. The other messages were scattered throughout the city—East Side, West Side, and Midtown. So, I've decided to focus on this group." Omar used the mouse to draw a circumference around the black dots clustered together. "Based on the information you've given me; this tower is within blocks of Olivia's apartment."

"So that doesn't tell us much. This doesn't mean Olivia's stalker lives near her. It could mean he's standing outside her place when he's sending this crap."

"But the IP address is different on all the messages."

"Can you track that them to a physical place?"

"They're hidden behind multiple layers of encryption. It's like trying to untangle a string of Christmas lights. If you made some calls, you'd get some answers a lot faster than I would."

"I'll get on it." Xander dropped his chin into his palm. "There's a lot of information here. You've done a good job, Omar."

Omar nodded. "Oh yeah. About our other work. You know, what we do when you're not falling in love? I've gotten a few calls." He shuffled through some papers. "My preliminary investigation says these are good assignments. Not like that scum, Popev. All of them are in the States. We'd be away for several weeks."

"In the States—I could do that." Xander rubbed the stubble on his chin. He'd planned to trim up after taking Olivia to the airport. Afterward, it hardly seemed necessary. "Give me the addresses of Olivia's friend David, her two assistants, and anybody else she calls in New York. These messages are coming from someone who must live in the city. Her stalker wouldn't go to New York to harass her electronically if he didn't live there."

CHAPTER 36

*T*he studio felt as welcoming as her apartment. There was comfort in the familiarity. Olivia unpacked the camera bag, checking her gear before Ajay and Gwen arrived. Getting to work early was supposed to give her time to clear her head and get back in work mode, but if two days alone at home hadn't cleared her head, nothing would. Sebastian Island was behind her, and so was Xander Fitzgerald. At least he'd been honest with her. She had to give him props for that. Most guys would have said they'd call or show up and then wouldn't.

Everyone wanted honesty until what they heard broke their heart.

She flipped through the pictures she and Xander had taken on the beach. They were supposed to be pretending, but she had never been more present. Those pictures from paradise would mark a time when she'd had everything she wanted, even if it'd been only make-believe.

"Hey, boss lady. You look like you had a good vacation." Ajay strolled toward her and planted a kiss on her cheek. "Where did you go?"

"I'm surprised to see you so early." She glanced at her phone. "You didn't need to be here for another hour."

"I get restless when I have too much time on my hands." He sighed. "Where'd you go?"

"A small island I used to go to when I was a little girl. How about you? Did you enjoy your week away?"

He sat on the bench beside her. "I stayed local. Spent a few days on Fire Island. It feels good to get the gang back together. Maybe we can go out after the shoot for a drink or something."

"Yeah, we'll see when Gwen gets here. Since you're here, you can go ahead and get those lights set up. We're shooting kids pictures today for a table book, so we're going to need some softer lights."

"Sure, boss."

"Don't call me that. I hate it. Why do you keep doing it?"

He gave a quick shrug. "You *are* the boss of this operation, and you *are* a lady."

"Yeah, but the way you say it sounds derogatory. I find the jobs, but we all work together." Having to explain to him set her back teeth on edge. She didn't want a boss, nor did she want to be considered one. That the reason she'd dropped out of graduate school and refused to work in a corporate job.

"My bad, Olivia. No harm intended." He brushed his hands together as if to say the conversation was finished. He moved across the room and started positioning the lights.

The only sound was the noise Ajay made while he worked. In just a few minutes the models would arrive. The flash would start clicking, and the world would continue to rotate on its axis. Today was a continuation of yesterday and the day before. Nobody would know that her life now had a period in it. Last week with Xander was a mark in time like no other for her.

"Hey, hey, hey. The gang's all here." Gwen walked into the studio with her signature duffle bag dangling from her arm. She wore a multi-color maxi dress that billowed around her like a soft cloud. She had one exposed shoulder. She could have been the one they were taking pictures of today.

Olivia closed her eyes for a moment. How could she forget their friendly fashion competition? Today she'd dressed in leggings. There was nothing special about her outfit just like there was nothing special about her disposition.

Gwen wrapped her in a warm embrace. "I missed you. And I want to hear all about your vacation later today. Ajay texted me and said we're all going out after the shoot."

Olivia didn't reply. Since when was Ajay calling the shots for the two of them?

CHAPTER 37

*O*livia glanced around the bar. The crowd was getting thicker. The noise level in the bar grew louder with each new patron that pressed into the small space. Being wedged on one side of the booth beside Ajay, with Gwen seated across the table, had been fun, but the solitude of her apartment called. It was going to take more than a few slightly dirty martinis to make her feel as jovial as her two assistants.

She glanced down at her phone again. The messages from Xander were like a neon light grabbing her attention.

"Why do you keep looking at your phone?" Ajay nudged her with his elbow.

"Yeah, what's going on over there?" Gwen tried to peek.

Olivia tucked her phone back into her purse. "I'm going to call it a night, guys. The tab's on me." Olivia placed her credit card on the table.

"Let's have one more. What's the rush?" Ajay slurred his words.

Gwen leaned across the table and said in a loud whisper, "I've got to run, too. I've met someone."

"Why did you wait so long to say something?" Olivia asked.

"We'll talk later this week." Gwen moved to slide out of the bench. "He could be the one. I'll have to fill you in. My Uber is outside." She waved before dashing out.

Olivia signaled for the check and slipped her card to the server without looking at the bill.

"What's your hurry? Just because Gwen's gone, we can stay. I'm enjoying myself," Ajay said.

"I'm ready to go home, Ajay."

He sighed loud enough for everyone sitting nearby to hear. "I'll walk you home."

"You don't have to do that. It's just a few blocks."

"I don't mind. I'm just not ready to head in yet." He stood to allow her to get out of the booth.

The server returned with her card. She signed the check, shoved the card into the side of her bag, then signaled Ajay she was ready to go.

Compared to the temperature on Sebastian Island, the summer heat in Queens was hotter and stickier. The weariness in her bones had nothing to do with hard work or overexertion. The drag came from carrying around the wound from Xander's words. He'd called earlier during her shoot, but she wasn't sure if talking to him was worthwhile. There was nothing to be gained by hearing his voice.

At the entrance to her building, she turned to Ajay. "Thank you for walking me home, Ajay." She gave him a quick hug.

"I've had a bit too much to drink, Olivia. Is your sofa open tonight?"

She eyed him. Having him in the apartment would keep her from calling Xander or moping around and feeling sorry for herself. Between the noise of the television and Ajay's love of hearing his own voice, she would have the perfect distractions.

"Okay, Ajay. On the sofa, just for the night."

"Of course. But tell me you have vodka, vermouth, and a few blue cheese-stuffed olives."

She looped her arm through his. "Even when I have nothing else in my house to eat, I always have the foundation for a good martini."

They climbed the stairs to her condo. "I appreciate this, Olivia. You know I missed you while you were away."

"I missed you guys, too. But from now on when we're putting together the shot calendar for the year, we'll have to make sure to allow at least a week of downtime."

Once inside, she motioned to the sofa. "There's your spot. I'm going to put my stuff away. Then we can make a few drinks,"

In her bedroom, she removed her slacks and tank to slip into a pair of Capri leggings with an oversized T-shirt. She walked out of the bedroom with her phone in her hand to find Ajay seated on the sofa, staring at his hands folded in front of him. His backpack was on the floor between his feet.

"Are you ready to mix a few martinis?"

Ajay looked up as if he hadn't expected her to leave the bedroom so soon. He jumped up from the sofa. "Yeah, right."

"You know where everything is." Olivia settled into the chair by the window. She stared at her phone, wanting to say something to Xander, but what? After formulating the words in her head all day, she was ready to send the text.

Xander, I didn't listen to your messages on purpose. I can accept that you think last week was a one-time deal. Thank you for the amazing time.

She reread the words before hitting the Send icon. Her eyes stung, but she refused to give in to the emotion swelling in her heart. "Where are the drinks?"

Ajay came her way carrying one in each hand. "Here." He handed one to her, then returned to his seat on the sofa. "You've been staring at your phone all day. What the hell is going on with you?"

"I met someone while I was away." She couldn't find the words to tell him more. "Let me show you some of the pictures we took last week." She retrieved the camera bag and removed the camera. Seated next to Ajay, she strolled through the pictures, skipping over the racy photos that needed too much explanation.

"Is this something serious?"

"No. I mean, I wish it could be. I think I love Xander. But, you know the long-distance thing…" She stared at the camera. Xander's dark eyes stared back at her, bringing back all the joy of last week.

"I didn't even know you were interested in dating anyone right now. I thought you were taking a break." The intensity of Ajay's voice edged up. His nostrils flared.

"Enough about me. Are you dating anyone?"

He slammed his glass down onto the table, sloshing the contents over the edge and breaking the stem on the glass.

Olivia leaped out of the chair. "Ajay, what is wrong with you? Are you drunk?"

"Hell no, Olivia. I'm not drunk. I'm pissed. You've been stringing me along for over three years. If you were ready to date, why aren't you dating me? You have to know how I feel about you." He stood and looked taller than usual.

Within an instant, heat encased her body. The man she thought she knew was not the man standing in front of her now. The only thing missing from Ajay's appearance was a gun, and he could have been one of the intruders in Xander's place.

"Ajay, let's talk about this. We work together. We are not going to be a couple. I made that very clear." Her voice was high, almost squeaky, but she tried to use a calming tone. He was powerful enough to rip her in two.

"I was giving you time. But I think you enjoy teasing me. Stringing me along like I'm some puppy." He hissed the words without moving his teeth.

She pulled in a deep breath, but the air wasn't enough to minimize the alarms sounding in her head. Fear gripped her throat, making it hard to form words. "Ajay." She spoke slowly. Deliberate. "Are you...the...person...who's...has... been...stalking me?"

He rushed to her side so fast, she flinched.

His face turned redder, he seemed to expand in size. "Stalking you? Are you fucking kidding me?" Spit flew from the corner of his mouth. "I am not a stalker. I've been in love with you for three years. Sending you signals that you've ignored." He clenched his fists.

"Ajay, we had a conversation about this. Don't you remember?"

"I'm not stupid, Olivia. Of course, I remember. You did all the talking. I don't think you heard anything I had to say. I've been sending you flowers, texts, notes. But I think I have your attention now, don't I?" He stood in front of her. His eyes were wide, daring her to say what he didn't want to hear. He snorted like a bull.

She had to remain calm. Ajay wouldn't hurt her, would he? She eased into the chair. With her back against the cushion, she tried to modulate the fear racing through every part of her body. There had to be something she could say or do to de-escalate this situation. Her heart pumped too fast, it was hard to think. "I'm sorry you don't think I took you seriously. I thought it was best for both of us to be friends, and not—" She couldn't say the word *lovers*. "Nothing more." She wanted to stand. Maybe if she was standing, she could intimidate him enough to back up. But his body was like a slab of concrete.

His eyes iced over, but he didn't say anything. She glanced around the room without moving. There had to be a way to make him think about this with a clearer head. The pepper spray was in her bag in the bedroom. There was no way she could get it now.

The long stretch of silence grew uncomfortable. Ajay wasn't calming down. With each breath, he became more intense. The quiet seemed to feed his psychosis. Beads of sweat peppered his forehead even though the apartment was cooler than usual.

"I think you should head home, Ajay." She moved to the edge of the chair.

He slammed the heels of his hands into her chest, knocking her back. "You're not calling the shots right now, boss lady. This time, I am. And I'm not going home. We're a couple, and it's about time you start to act like it." He grabbed the neck of her top, ripping the thin fabric and exposing her breast.

She smacked him so hard her palm throbbed. Shock registered on his face followed by anger. He grabbed her breasts and squeezed them hard.

She yelled as the pain shot through her body. She had to stop him. She smacked his right cheek, then his left, in quick succession with all her strength. He released her breasts but continued to stand over her. She could feel each of his breaths. "Ajay, think about what you're doing. Are you going to rape me? You're not this guy."

He grabbed her by the hair and yanked her out of the chair. Her scalp screamed from the torture as if it was being separated from her head. Trying to break away from him increased the agony. Her feet barely touched the floor as he yanked her across the room. With each step he took, he pulled her hair harder. She clawed at his hands, scratching and hitting, but he was unaffected.

The pounding of her heart vibrated in her ears. She had to do something, but he was in a trance, oblivious to the torment he was inflicting. This was how murders happened. He wasn't aware of his actions. If he killed her or raped her, it would haunt him forever. She knew that much about him or at least she thought she did.

Her heart sped up. "Ajay, stop. She tried to wiggle free. "Stop it." She smacked him, but it was as effective as swatting flies. She needed to get his attention. "Ajay, think about what you're doing." She shouted as loud as she could.

He stopped at her bedroom door, shook her like a rag doll, then shoved her inside. He pinned her down on the bed and backhanded her across the cheek before he tore at her leggings. His eyes were vacant.

CHAPTER 38

$\mathcal{X}$ander looked out the window of the taxi. Queens was lusher and high-end than he'd imagined. His time in New York was all spent in Manhattan, but he could understand why Olivia lived here. The neighborhood was vibrant and effervescent just like her.

He wasn't supposed to miss her as much as he did, but while everything ticked along just like life intended, snatches of Olivia kept popping up. He could still smell her cologne, feel her touch, and hear the timbre of her voice whispering in his ear when he was supposed to be sleeping.

That's what he was running from. But instead of running *toward* Olivia, he'd pushed her away. Maybe Hope was right, and he *was* warped in some ways he didn't even understand. But, at least now, he could be the hero Olivia needed. He was worthy. A few phone calls, a little snooping, and the secret behind her stalker was there.

"This is your stop." The driver pulled up to a building with a green awning.

"Thanks, man." Xander patted the front seat and climbed

out. He processed the view before going inside. At the entrance, he pulled his cell phone from his pocket. The text she'd sent a few moments ago stared back at him. Even though her words weren't angry—as a matter of fact, her words were on the sunny side of pleasant—there was fury buried in every letter. And he deserved each and every degree.

He dialed her number. The phone rang twice before she picked up. But she didn't say hello.

"Olivia, are you there?" he asked. "It's me, Xander. I'm in New York and I want to see you."

The only sound on the other end was breathing.

"Olivia, I just want to talk. I have something important to share. Will you buzz me up?"

Still no answer.

Something wasn't right. Maybe she didn't want to talk to him, but Olivia would have said so. Speaking her mind wasn't her problem. He pulled up his notes on Olivia to find the name of her cop friend here in New York.

When he located the name, he dialed David.

"David. I think Olivia is in trouble." He blurted out the words.

"Who the hell is this?"

"Xander, her friend from Sebastian Island. I'm here in New York outside her building and when I dialed her number all I got was heavy breathing."

"Maybe she doesn't want to talk to you. Maybe she's busy."

Xander held up his index finger as if David could see the gesture. "I dialed her number. Someone picked up, but it wasn't her. I think she's in trouble. I can't get into the building."

David didn't respond.

Xander waited a second. "I need to be sure she's okay.

What's the code to get into the building?" He was yelling now.

"I'm on my way."

"I can't wait for you. Give me the damn code, now."

"You had better not be bullshitting me, man." He provided the code. "I'll be there in five minutes."

Xander pushed the code into the keypad. In the lobby, he looked around for the elevator. There wasn't one, so he sprinted up the three flights. This was not one of those ring-the-doorbell moments. He pulled the kit from his duffel and inserted the tension wrench into the bottom of the lock, then he pushed the pick into the top of the lock, scrubbed it back and forth until the tumblers dropped. Then he withdrew the Glock from his bag and eased the door open.

CHAPTER 39

Olivia's arms flailed across the bed. All she needed to do was get her hands on her purse. She needed the pepper spray.

If Ajay hadn't been drunk, ripping her leggings away would have only taken a minute. Instead, he tried to pull the fabric over her hips. Without her assistance, he struggled. He leaned toward her and tried to push his tongue into her mouth. She clamped her teeth because his nauseating breath turned her stomach.

From the living room, her cell phone rang—The Merrymen's *Feeling hot, hot, hot,* the song she'd selected as Xander's ringtone. Oh, God, she needed him now.

The sound snapped Ajay's head up. He rushed out of the room. The phone stopped ringing midway through the third time, so she figured he must have answered it.

She jumped up and locked the bedroom door.

Men wanted to control her life. Every aspect of it. Her father, her brothers, to one extreme, David and Xander trying so hard to protect her they left her almost helpless, and now Ajay. Heat emanated from her skin. Standing up for herself wasn't something she'd ever done, but what better time? If she couldn't take control of her life now, then she never would. She found her bag on the floor beside the bed. Ajay was coming back. She removed her office keys and inserted a key between each of her fingers. Then she dug out the pepper spray. Ajay might expect it, but he wouldn't expect her to take out his eyes.

"Oh, Olivia, your boyfriend called." Ajay sang the words as if they were in a psychological thriller. He was back at the bedroom door, turning the knob.

"Open the door, Olivia." His voice was sickeningly sweet.

"You've had a lot to drink, go home."

"Don't tell me how much to drink. How does it feet to have someone tell you what to do, boss lady?" He pounded on the door. "Now open this damn door or I'll kick it in."

She inhaled a deep breath and held it. With her hands behind her back, Ajay wouldn't see what she had waiting for him. "GO HOME, AJAY!"

Ajay's leather shoe came through the door. Wood and hardware sprayed everywhere. The crash was louder than she'd imagine. He stumbled inside, lunging for her again. His eyes dead. He fell on top of her throwing her onto the bed. He shoved his hands into the waistband of her leggings. Before he could get between her legs, she jammed the keys toward his eyes. She missed, but several keys went into his nostrils. She rolled away from him.

"You bitch!" He seized her tattered leggings and ripped them more. She doused him in pepper spray. He let go of her and covered his eyes. "Aghhhhhhh!"

She charged out of the bedroom and through the apartment, but before she reached the front door, Xander stepped through it.

CHAPTER 40

*X*ander rubbed his hands together as the police took Ajay away in handcuffs. Olivia had run into his arms when she'd first seen him, but there was a definite frost in the room now. He couldn't help staring at her. She looked the same, maybe more beautiful, but her hands shook, and she wouldn't let him touch her now.

Those few minutes with her body pressed against his had been a wakeup call he hadn't known he'd needed.

"Are you sure you're okay, Olivia?" David asked.

"I'm fine. I'll be bruised and sore tomorrow, but for now, I'm fine. I'm just glad the whole ordeal is over. It's over." Tears appeared in her eyes. "I never thought Ajay would do something like that. He was…He was unrecognizable." She placed her hand over her mouth.

"You can sleep well tonight, knowing your stalker is behind bars." David stood and held his hand out to Xander. "It was nice to meet you. Thanks for the heads-up."

"Thanks for trusting me with the code. But I think our girl was going to be okay without our help. By the time I got to Ajay, he was begging for help and wanted to get away from Oliva."

The two of them chuckled.

"I'm glad the two of you can see the brighter side of my disaster." She fell back against the chair and stared at the ceiling.

"We're just teasing you, Olivia. But you did put a big hurt on the guy," David said.

"He deserved everything he got. I should have cracked his nuts," she said while continuing to contemplate something on the ceiling only she could see.

David kissed her cheek. "I'll check in with you tomorrow. Call me if you need me."

"I always do," she said before waving goodbye.

David closed the door behind him, leaving Xander alone with her.

For several moments neither of them said anything. Various forms of an apology raced through his head.

"I can't believe Ajay did all those things. The way he stared at me tonight. The way he talked to me. I find it hard to link that to the man I thought I knew."

"People let you see the parts they want you to see. If you could read minds, you'd be quite surprised."

"When did you find out it was Ajay?"

"Two days ago. As soon as I figured it out, I leased a plane to bring me to New York."

"I guess I should thank you."

"I wish you would stop staring at the ceiling and look at me."

She took her time, but she tilted her head just enough for him to see her face.

"I'm sorry for all those things I said our last day together."

She shook her head. "Don't be. You told your truth.

There's no way I can be mad at a man for telling the truth. It's the ones who lie to me that get me riled up."

"I didn't mean to mislead you."

"I probably made the mistake every woman makes at some point. The setting was idealistic, you're handsome, the food was delicious, so in my mind, I took all that, stirred it together, and swore there were wedding bells in our future." She waved her hand in a dismissive gesture. "I got carried away—something I'd promised myself I wasn't going to do again.

He pushed off the sofa and made his way to the window. She didn't have much of a view. Across the street was another building, just as tall as hers, and just as unimpressive. Living in the city had its benefits, but he needed a little more space, a little more quiet, and room to roam.

With his back to her, he said, "I really like you, Olivia." He paused long enough to doubt what he was getting ready to say next. He could head back to Sebastian and continue to live his life, but couldn't fit into the cocoon he'd created for himself anymore. "I was wrong about us. I want more."

She didn't respond. Her breathing didn't even change. He wanted to turn around and look at her, but in case she wasn't in the mood to forgive him, he hesitated.

"You're just saying that. The last few weeks have been a roller coaster ride. Who knows what we're feeling or thinking?"

He faced her. "Don't blow me off Olivia. Adrenaline rushes are what I do for a living. What happened in Sebastian with Jacob was a play-date for me. I may not have been thinking straight when you left, but I've had plenty of time to get my act together." He swallowed. "I'm in love with you, Olivia."

She glanced at him. He had her full attention, but her face didn't change. He waited a moment for her to say something.

She didn't.

"Are you going to pretend you didn't hear me?"

She stood. "Yeah. That's exactly what I'm going to do. Goodnight."

CHAPTER 41

The only thing missing from Olivia's stroll out of the room—*away* from Xander—was the ability to slam her bedroom door. The hinges and the latch on the door hung sadly, thanks to Ajay.

She fell across the bed. If her body weren't so tired, she would have been willing to word volley with Xander for a few more hours. But when he slammed the "I'm in love with you" comment right into her face, she realized she didn't have the necessary stamina. Not after the day she'd had. What was she supposed to do with *I love you*? Forget about everything else? And what if the relationship blew up once she was all—in? Wouldn't everyone say, *he told you he wasn't ready, why didn't you believe him?*

She turned onto her other side, putting her back to the broken door. She should have been relieved that the big mystery in her life was solved. But instead, she was numb or at least she wanted to be. Pushing away her feelings was a lot easier than trying to decipher Xander's.

"Olivia." He knocked on the wall.

"Yes?" She didn't turn toward him.

His footsteps were light as he came into the room. The mattress sagged under his weight when he sat on it. "I meant what I said. If I hadn't been trying so hard to ignore what was happening between us, I would have said how I felt before you left."

She sat up against the pillow and faced him. "Xander, what am I supposed to do with that?" Her voice was flat. She couldn't rally for another round. "Do I come off so desperate that no matter what you say or do, I'll be sitting here panting hoping you'll throw me something to hold on to?" She grabbed her hair, but quickly let it go. Her scalp still throbbed from Ajay's action.

"Oh, my God. This must have been how Ajay felt. Is this what I did to him? Did I jerk him around because I couldn't get myself together?"

"This is nothing like Ajay." Xander rubbed his forehead. "I'm telling you what's in my heart." He reached for her hands, squeezed them just enough to convey some emotions. "I wanted to take my time. I didn't want to jump in and realize I was hasty. I've spent every minute since you left Sebastian thinking about you. Thinking about us. I know, without a doubt, that I love you. That I want to be with you. I'd prefer to be with you in Sebastian, but if it has to be New York, then I'll pack up and move here. I don't care where we are as long as I'm with you."

She couldn't fight it anymore. Standing on the side of right didn't feel as fabulous as standing on the side of love. Just once, she wanted someone to walk with her through the maze. She exhaled all the doubt, and, thought about the possibility—the what if.

"I love you too, Xander."

CHAPTER 42

Olivia propped her feet up on the rail of the deck and stared down the hill at the waves lapping the Sebastian shore. A cool breeze pushed her natural hair to one side and covered her face. October on Sebastian Island was just as beautiful as June, minus the heat, and with a little less humidity.

"We're going to do this, right?" Xander came through the French doors carrying two glasses of wine.

"I think we are, sweetheart." She held up her hand to stare at the large diamond he'd placed on her finger. "I've never been a frilly girl, but I love the ring, and the size certainly makes a statement."

He kissed her forehead. "I love it when you call me sweetheart. Nothing sounds better to my ears." He handed her a glass, and then pressed another kiss to her neck. "Aren't your parents going to be upset if we don't do the traditional wedding thing—the church, the white dress, long train, and the big stuffy reception in somebody's country club?"

She sipped the wine. "It's taken me a long time to become the person I'm happy with." She pulled him down into the chair next to her. "And I have to thank you for helping to set me free. Once we set a date, my parents will be here. Sebastian is my home now. You are the center of my life. My dad will walk me across the sand and into your arms because he loves me. He might not be happy with the way we're choosing to do this, but he'll be here."

"Was he upset when he found out you wanted to live here with me?"

"He was upset when I moved to New York, so, he's getting used to the idea that he can't tell me what to do. We'll be in the States often enough to appease him and my mother. I still have my work."

"Do they think we're moving too fast?"

She put her glass down to hold his face. "It's been over a year. We're not getting married tomorrow, so we're not rushing. I'm surprised you took this long to ask me. I was beginning to think you were getting cold feet again."

"I wanted to wait until the Ajay thing was over. If he hadn't pleaded guilty, you would have had to wait even longer. I didn't want him hanging over your decision."

"I don't want to talk about him or think about him." She lifted her head, pushing away the memory of that night. "Anyway, my family adores you just like I do. My father thinks you're some macho man who will protect his daughter."

"He's right you know. I am a macho man, and I *will* protect his daughter."

"And I'll protect you." She slipped her tongue into his mouth.

UP NEXT

EXCERPT FROM

<u>TROUBLE IN PARADISE</u>

*L*awrence Cistos eased into the sturdy chair behind his desk. His ample backside hung over the sides, but no one dared comment on his girth or his attitude. Both needed an adjustment, but, in his line of work, these characteristics were beneficial. When his size didn't intimidate his opponent, then his attitude did.

He looked across the mahogany desk at the two men sitting in front of him. They appeared adequate for his purposes. Between the two of them, there were enough muscles to supply a small army.

Lawrence cleared his throat. "This meeting will be short. You're aware of my expectations. You've been briefed. Kais Bisset has assured me the painting arrived on Sebastian Island, and the tracking device I had installed verifies the same thing. It's in some warehouse unit guarded by a company owned by some expert named Xander Fitzgerald. Fitzgerald's good, but you guys are supposed to be better. Based on my last conversation with Kais, he's backing out of the deal because he thinks he can get more for the painting. He obviously doesn't know me or my reputation. I want that corrected." Lawrence allowed the anger in his gut to fill his voice.

"We're ready, Lawrence. Give us the signal."

"This meeting is the damn signal. Did you think you're here for a fucking tea party?" Lawrence studied the men. He didn't know either of their names and had never met them, but if things went according to the plan, he would never see them again, so it wouldn't matter. He just wanted a job done, and these two came recommended. There were no calls, text or emails connecting the two of them to him. Discretion was the cornerstone of his business.

"I want you to find my painting, and I want the print behind the frame. I've been a patient man, but I have my limits." Lawrence pounded the desk. "Kais is stupid and greedy and well out of his league if he thinks he can negotiate with me. We had a deal. He's made an unfortunate error."

Both men pushed to the edge of their chairs. Their unison movements and head nodding had to be something they practiced.

Lawrence slid the fat, white envelope across the desk. "Here's the retainer. You'll get the balance when I get my painting and print. As long as the print is in mint condition."

The guy who sat closest to the desk reached for the envelope, extracted the cash and threaded the bills through his fingers. Afterward, he shoved the package into the breast pocket of his suit jacket. "Are there any limitations on how far we can go?"

Lawrence stood and pointed his finger at the one doing the talking. "I want my painting and print back intact. I don't care about Kais Bisset or anyone else. I've shelled out good money. If someone gets in the way, handle it. That's what I'm paying for."

ABOUT THE AUTHOR

Jacki Kelly has written dozens of short stories and several books. She lives in the Northeast with her husband and one loveable dog. She loves hearing from her readers, so please contact her.

Connect with her online:
http://www.jackikelly.com
Twitter - @jackikellybooks
http://facebook.com/jackikellyauthor

If you enjoyed reading Pictures from Paradise, please tell everyone you know, and please post a review for other readers on your favorite reading forum.